Camp All-Star

Michael Coldwell

shawty

James Lorimer & Company, Publishers
Toronto, 1996

James Lorimer & Company Ltd. acknowledges with thanks the support of the Canada Council and the Ontario Arts Council in the development of writing and publishing in Canada.

Cover illustration: Ian Watts

Canadian Cataloguing in Publication Data

Coldwell, Michael
Camp all-star

(Sports stories)
ISBN 1-55028-527-0 (bound) ISBN 1-55028-526-2 (pbk.)

I. Title. II. Series: Sports stories (Toronto, Ont.).

PS8555.04326C35 1996   jC813'.54   C96-931781-6
PZ7.C65Ca 1996

James Lorimer & Company Ltd., Publishers
35 Britain Street
Toronto, Ontario
M5A 1R7

Printed and bound in Canada

Contents

To Mom and Dad

1

Crazy Chip Carson

This is going to be cool, I thought as I hauled my enormous duffle bag out of the car and turned to gaze at the grey stone building that would be my home for the next two weeks. Fourteen days of nothing but hard-core basketball with some of the best players in the entire province. The parking lot was buzzing with other boys calling their goodbyes as they were dropped off at the Dalhousie University summer basketball camp.

If my stepmother hadn't tried to hug me, things would have been perfect.

"C'mon, Jeff," Sharon cooed, "give me a hug. I'm going to miss you, honey."

"Sharon, I'm only going for two weeks," I said, fending off her embrace. "Besides, you've got that convention in town anyway. It's not like I'm going to be a thousand miles away."

"No matter," Sharon dismissed my protest and kissed me hard on the cheek. Yuck. How embarrassing. I stumbled backward and turned to see if anyone had noticed. Fortunately, the other guys were too busy dodging kisses from their own parents to notice me.

"Now, here's the number of the hotel I'm staying at," Sharon continued, thrusting a slip of paper into my hand. "If you need anything just call. I don't know what my meeting schedule is like, but if I'm not too busy maybe I'll drop by and see how you're getting along." Sharon hopped into the car and drove off.

That was exactly what I was afraid of.

Every summer, basketball players ages fourteen and up came from all across Nova Scotia to the campus of Dalhousie University for a two-week basketball skills camp. The hoop camp taught a young player everything from the basics of dribbling to complex defensive strategies, with lots of competition in between. The whole idea made me almost drool.

A light breeze swept across the laneway as I walked towards the Howe Hall residence building. The wind would have made my hair wave, except for the fact that I got it all chopped off two days before; shaved "right down to the wood," as my dad said. I also had five pounds of new muscles from a serious weight-training program. It was scary, but I almost looked like a basketball player, no small feat for a guy barely standing five foot two.

Don't be fooled by my height, though. I'm a serious player. I capped off last season as the starting guard for the Bridgewater High junior varsity team, and my coach even hinted that I may have a spot on the senior team next year, even though I will still only be fourteen. I smiled to myself — no kidding, I was a basketball player. Now all I had to do was show my stuff to Coach Don Demchyshyn.

Coach Demchyshyn — or Coach D. as he was often called for obvious reasons — was the director of the camp. Although he was getting on in years, he was still considered the best basketball mind in the province. I had read and reread the write-up on Coach D. in the camp brochure until I had it practically memorized. I knew everything there was to know about the man except what he liked to eat for dinner. Coach Demchyshyn had spent over twenty years coaching the game of basketball. Now for the last four years Coach D. had been running the Dalhousie hoop camp and coaching the Nova

Scotia Juvenile All-Star Team. It was this last point on Coach D.'s impressive résumé that I found most interesting.

Coach D. would be scouting players for his all-star squad during the camp. At the end of the two weeks, he would select the twelve best players, who would then go to Ontario to play against other provincial rep teams in a huge tournament. I was almost positive that I was good enough to make the all-star team. In fact I was tempted to tell the coach what size uniform I wore so it would be ready for me when my name was called.

Reaching the end of the walkway, I entered the dormitory where all the players would stay. The lobby was packed with parents and campers milling about like ants. Everyone was shouting and waving room keys and camp T-shirts. To my left was a long table where people seemed to be checking in.

"Name please?" asked the tired-looking girl working the desk as I slipped my way into the crowd.

"Jeff Lang."

The frazzled attendant handed me a brown envelope and a black-and-gold camp T-shirt. "Here's your information package. You're in room 121. It's up the stairs at the end of the hall."

I opened my mouth to ask a question.

"Next!" called the attendant, and I was squished out of the crowd like a wet watermelon seed.

As I sauntered up the stairs I noticed a boy unsuccessfully trying to duck his mother's farewell kiss. I was glad my stepmom had dropped me off in the parking lot.

After my dad remarried, Sharon and I couldn't stay in the same room for more than two minutes without yelling at each other. Now, almost a year later, she'd pulled a complete one-eighty. She was always kissing and hugging me and calling me cutesy names. It was better than fighting, I guess, but at fourteen I was getting too big for all the kissy stuff.

Moving through the narrow upstairs corridor I peeked in a few open doors and noticed that the dorm rooms were all pretty similar. Two single beds, two dressers, two desks and a window in the middle. In most rooms guys were unpacking their shorts and T-shirts and getting to know their new room-mate.

Loud rap music pumped through the hallway and I felt like I was set on cruise control. I was relieved to notice that I wasn't that much smaller than most of the other guys.

It was going to be a great two weeks, I decided as I reached the door of room 121. Away from home for fourteen days of hard-nosed basketball — what could go wrong?

As I pushed open the door I had my answer.

"Hey there, Roomie!"

I was knocked speechless.

Room 121 — my room — was completely filled with ... junk. Suitcases, clothes, shoes and CDs were strewn everywhere. All four walls were completely plastered with posters of guys on mountain bikes. There was an assortment of helmets, gloves and strange-looking tools on what should have been my bed, and to eat up the last little bit of space, there was a bright green mountain bike propped up in the very centre of the room.

"Hey, I was wondering when you were going to show up, man."

The sentence came from a guy about my size with wild orange hair, a bright tie-dyed T-shirt and black spandex shorts. He was jumping up and down on the bed and grooving to music being injected into his skull from a pair of enormous headphones.

I was still unable to speak so the boy continued talking. "I'm Chip Carson," he said, bouncing over and vigorously shaking my hand. "Glad to meet you."

I didn't know where this guy had come from, but he had managed to totally shatter my cool in about three seconds. "I'm Jeff Lang ..." I mumbled, frantically searching for something else to say. "Um, all this stuff ..." I gestured helplessly at the mass of clutter filling the tiny room.

"Yeah, I know," Chip said apologetically. "But I've only been here for a couple of hours. In a few days we'll really give it that lived-in look."

"And the bike ..." I continued, dazed.

"It's pretty cool, huh? It's a Shimanto 150 EXL hybrid-racer with graphite frame, titanium shocks, high-performance gears and a special scratch-resistant day-glo paint job." Chip shook his head. "Would you believe they actually wanted me to keep that baby outside?"

I believed it.

"Anyway, this camp is going to be awesome, huh? We are going to have a totally rocking time. I can feel it! A whole two weeks with no parents, just hanging out with the guys and having fun! Too cool," Chip babbled excitedly.

"And basketball," I reminded my strange roommate.

"Oh yeah, I guess we'll have to do some of that, won't we?" Chip frowned.

I managed to clear a spot on the floor and set down my duffle bag. Letting out a long sigh, I tried to remember what I had done to deserve this.

"Hey, is there a Chip Carson in here?" called a dark-haired boy who peeked in from the doorway.

"Yep, that's me," Chip said. "What's up?"

"Hall phone's for you. It's your parents." The boy disappeared around the corner.

"My folks," Chip groaned. "They just left me here a couple of hours ago and they're checking up on me already! Un-be-lievable!" Chip rolled his eyes and hurried out of the room.

I flopped onto a corner of the bed, which was remarkably free of clothes, CDs, posters and bike accessories, and nodded my head miserably. Chip Carson was, indeed, unbelievable.

Lying down, I stared at the ceiling and tried to clear my head. Much to my dismay, Chip had covered it with biking posters as well. This guy was a fanatic.

Still a little unsettled, I rolled over on my stomach and started leafing through my camp information package. I had only turned a few pages when Chip blew back into the room.

"Man, my folks drive me nuts," he cried, running his fingers through his mat of orange hair. "Get this — my mom just told me to dress warmly — dress warmly — hello! It's July! How many people get pneumonia in July?" He shook his head. "Parents, geez. How about you, Jeff? Your folks drive you nuts too?"

I nodded absently.

"Get this — I'm from Cape Breton, right, and my folks finally agree to let me come to Halifax for this camp and then they come here during the same two weeks for a 'vacation'! How convenient! As if Captain Melonhead here wouldn't catch on to their little ploy."

I could relate. "My stepmom's here too. She has some convention. I'm sure she'll drop by sooner or later. Probably sooner. Anyway," I said, putting an end to the chit-chat, "we should get going. We've got the camp opening ceremonies to go to."

"Yeah, can you wait a few minutes?" Chip asked, grabbing a small strange-looking tool that looked like it had been stolen from a dentist's office. "I've just got to tighten up my spokes."

I didn't understand why Chip had to tighten his spokes before walking over to the gym, but I didn't feel like arguing.

"Well, we don't have that much time," I said pointedly.

"No hurry, man," Chip said casually. "I know a shortcut."

Ten minutes later Chip had finished tinkering with his bicycle and was leading me down a strange hallway. As we reached the rear exit of Howe Hall I couldn't help noticing that we seemed to be headed in the exact opposite direction of all the other campers. Despite my better judgement, I followed my roommate.

Chip wasn't very tall. In fact, he was slightly shorter than me but with tree trunks for legs. He walked with a little bounce and he constantly fidgeted with his hands, as if he was trying to burn off excess energy.

"The gym should be just around this corner," said Chip as we hustled down the sidewalk. Around the corner was a drugstore, a coffee shop and the large steel gates to the Halifax Public Gardens. There was, however, no gym.

"You sure about this shortcut?" I asked, slightly annoyed.

"I think so." Chip was bewildered. "I'll check my compass."

"Compass?"

Then, like something out of a James Bond movie, Chip popped the face off his watch to reveal a compass underneath.

"Nice gizmo."

"It's my biking watch," Chip explained, staring at the needle intently. "According to this, the gym should be just west of here," Chip said, pointing directly at the Public Gardens.

I had only been to Halifax a few times since I moved to Nova Scotia the previous year, but I was willing to bet that the Dalhousie gym wasn't in the middle of the Public Gardens.

"Wait here, Marco Polo," I said, as I spotted a young woman wearing a Dalhousie Law School T-shirt walking towards us. "I'm going to find out where the gym is."

It only took me a second to get the right directions. "Let's go," I said briskly. The gymnasium was ten minutes away in the opposite direction.

"Sorry about the mix-up, man," Chip said, tapping his wrist compass and looking a little sheepish.

"Hmmm," I fumed, glancing at my watch. It didn't have a compass in it, but it confirmed what I feared. We were late.

***

"Here at the Dalhousie summer basketball camp we pride ourselves on teaching teamwork, fundamentals and the value of hard work."

The speech echoed through the large domed structure that housed the Dalhousie gymnasium. Known as the Dalplex, the building actually contained several gyms, tennis courts, a weight room and a running track. Although the basketball court was almost in the centre of the structure, the words found their way to the furthest corners of the building. Weaving our way through several sets of stacked bleachers, Chip and I raced to track down the source. Taking a tight corner we burst onto the basketball court — ten minutes late and right in the middle of Coach Don Demchyshyn's annual welcoming address.

"Basketball is a team game, gentlemen. Five men working not as individuals, but firing as a single unit with a single goal. There is no 'I' in 'team.' Your teammates must be able to depend on you and you must depend on them," Coach D. intoned, catching a glimpse of Chip and me as we tried unsuccessfully to melt into the crowd of boys dotting the gym floor.

The coach stopped in mid-speech and focused his steel grey eyes on us. It was clear he was not happy about being interrupted. "Do you see what happens when we are not focused as a team, gentlemen?" Coach D. asked, gesturing our way. "When we are not focused, we experience distractions. And distractions will cause the downfall of any team. Now, if there are to be no more distractions, perhaps I may continue?"

Coach D. glared at us and after an awkward pause resumed his speech.

I felt about two feet tall. Sure, I wanted Coach D. to notice me, but certainly not like this.

"Sounds like someone needs a bit more fibre in their diet," hissed Chip, unfazed by the coach's remarks.

I glared at my roommate.

We took a seat near the back of the gym and I tried to enjoy the rest of the coach's speech. With a strong but even tone, his words made my ears perk up and pay extra attention. The man was a great speaker, and he could really get you motivated, that was for sure. Coach D.'s voice was low and gravelly, and he sounded as wise as he looked, with his penetrating grey eyes and silver hair brushed straight back.

The coach spoke for almost half an hour. That was a long time, but not one of the campers seemed restless. At the end of his talk the players were so fired up they could have held their own in the NBA.

Instead of starting the formal drills right away, Coach D. let us shoot around and play some pick-up games. We would get down to business tomorrow.

Still a little miffed at Chip for making me late, I was happy to blow off some steam shooting hoops. As I jogged to join a group of boys playing at one of the far baskets, I noticed Chip take a seat on the bleachers, whip out a magazine that had been tucked into his shorts and start to read. Weirdo.

"Quick game of threes?" called a tall, lanky boy collecting rebounds under the hoop.

The guys nodded their agreement, and it took only a minute to make two teams.

I slapped five with my teammates and made the brief introductions. Dan Oakie was over six feet tall and had a set of pipes on him that would make Mr. Universe jealous. "Call me 'Oak,'" Dan boomed in a thick Jamaican accent. With his size, I'd call him anything he wanted. My other teammate was a wiry guy named Scott Tran. Scott was wearing a silky black jersey, black shorts and enough gold chains around his neck to start his own jewellery store.

My team had the ball. I dribbled patiently at the top of the key and surveyed the situation. Scott's defender was playing him tough so I looked to the post to see what Oak was doing. Not surprisingly, Oak, like some sort of human bulldozer, had cleared out considerable space for himself and had his lanky defender neatly pinned behind him. Making the obvious play, I dumped a pass to Oak, who easily spun and thumped the backboard with two hands as he jumped up to power in the layup.

Scott took the ball at the top of the key and promptly zipped a pass to me as I spotted up on the wing. I was being guarded by a small boy with a roundish face and a bright orange T-shirt. Not wasting a second, I jab faked to get my man off balance and then let fly a feather-soft jump shot.

"Sweet," said Scott, letting out a low whistle as the ball swished the net. On the next play Scott fed me again, and this time I made a nifty cross-over dribble to burn by my defender before nailing a baseline jumper.

Still controlling the ball, my team proceeded to work it around looking for a good shot. When Scott pounded the ball into Oak he was quickly double-teamed so he kicked it out to me and I nailed another outside jump shot.

"Like money in the bank," called Scott, slapping five with me.

I tried to hide a smile. Three-for-three, I was red-hot and really feeling the rhythm. It was as if I could heave up any shot I wanted and it would go in. I especially loved playing hoops when I had that feeling.

I was busy thinking about the next way I could take my man to school, when Scott's defender came over and tapped his teammate on the arm. "Switch up," the solid boy instructed, "you take the guy in the black jersey, I'll take the shooter."

I sized up my new defender intently. He was taller than me and was dressed in a plain white T-shirt and white baggy shorts. He wasn't wearing any socks at all, and his brand new white sneakers almost glowed. Come to think about it, with light blond hair and a perfect smile, this whole kid seemed to glow.

"I'm Jay Best," the boy said amicably, extending his hand.

Reluctantly, I introduced myself and tapped Jay's hand slightly. I didn't like making friends with the competition during the game; especially when I was planning on shooting the lights out on this guy.

Taking the ball up top, Scott decided to go to my hot hand once more. Squaring up to the hoop, I faked right but Jay didn't buy it and kept right in my face. I tried to cross over my dribble and drive right, but Jay was too quick. He reached out and stole the ball from me.

"Let's not force it, huh, Jeff," called Oak. "I was open down there." He sounded a little annoyed. I nodded and thumped myself in the chest as if to say "my fault." The last thing I wanted was the reputation of being a ball hog.

Jay bounced the ball at the top of the circle and lobbed a pass to his lanky teammate who was battling for position against Oak. The skinny boy wheeled around and took a weak shot, which Oak promptly swatted into the next time zone.

"Get that garbage out of here," Oak bellowed, raising his arms in celebration and slapping a high-ten with Scott and me. The celebration was premature, however, because Jay had collected the rejected ball and was now speeding down the lane for an uncontested layup.

"Gotta tighten up the defence there, guys," Jay chided, flashing a good-natured smile.

I hung my head. I hated making mental mistakes like that. You can't stop concentrating in the middle of a game just because someone makes a nice play.

After the check, Jay started slowly dribbling the ball, looking for an opportunity to make something happen. Making his move, Jay did a wicked stutter step that left my knees feeling like Jell-o. Rocking on my heels, I was helpless as he breezed by me and soared in for another layup.

"Whoops, sorry about that," he cried, as he lightly stepped on my foot as he landed.

"No problem," I said through clenched teeth.

I had hardly handed the ball back to Jay before he nailed a quick jumper from the top of the key.

A little annoyed, I wasn't yet worried. My team was still ahead by a hoop. After Jay scored another two quick buckets to put us down by one, I was a little more concerned.

Jay was so quick off the dribble that I had to back off to give him some room, but when I did that he just knocked down the open jump shot.

What made me more mad was Jay's on-court chatter. He didn't talk trash — I could handle that — Jay was just a talker. He would say little things like, "good hustle," "nice try," or after he boxed me out fiercely, he'd ask, "you okay?" Jay was so friendly, it was like playing hoops against Barney the Purple Dinosaur.

Making another tough jump shot, Jay smiled. "That was a little lucky," he laughed.

After running off seven straight hoops, I knew that this guy wasn't lucky, this guy was good.

Slinking off the court in defeat, I weakly slapped five with my teammates.

"Sorry, I couldn't stop that guy," I said as I shook Oak's meaty hand.

"Don't worry about it, man," Oak said in his deep voice. "Jay is real good. He started for the all-star team last year."

"Really, did he tell you that?" I asked, perking up at the mention of the all-star squad.

"No, I played with him," said Oak.

"You made the team, too?" I exclaimed.

"Well, you don't have to sound so surprised about it," replied Oak, getting a little peeved. "I'm not bad, you know."

"Sorry," I said, embarrassed. "It's not that, I was just hoping that I could make that team, too."

"Yeah, you and everyone else here," piped in Scott.

"Only some of us have a better chance than others," joked Oak, slapping Scott in the arm. "I'm sort of an expert scout when it comes to the all-star team," Oak declared proudly. "If you need any inside information, just see me. I always know who Coach D. is looking at."

"How do you know that?" I asked, impressed.

"I'm afraid I can't reveal my sources," Oak replied slyly. "Anyway, me and Scotty are going to get something to eat. You wanna come along?"

I was a little hungry, but seeing Coach D. on the far sidelines I thought of something I had to do first. "You guys go ahead. I'll see you later."

As Oak and Scott left the gym, I made a beeline for Coach D. I figured that if I apologized for coming in late I might be able to get on the coach's good side.

"Tough game, huh?" came a voice from behind me. It was Chip.

"Are you still here? I thought you went back to the room."

"I would have but you have the room key," Chip replied, not sounding annoyed at all.

"Sorry." I fished the key out of my sock, handed it to Chip and kept walking towards Coach D.

"Are you coming?" asked Chip, hurrying after me.

"Yeah. I just want to talk to Coach D. first. You go ahead."

"Nah, I may as well wait for you," responded Chip brightly as he followed me over to where Coach D. was standing. "You don't mind, do you?"

I minded and later wished I had said so.

2

A Scientific Snob

How could you do that to me?" I yelled as Chip and I returned to our small dorm room. "Don't you even know who Coach Demchyshyn is?"

"I thought I was helping," replied Chip. "Didn't you want to get on his good side after walking in late and all?"

"You told him I was an exchange student from Sweden and couldn't tell time in Canada yet!" I hollered, feeling my face turn a light shade of purple.

"Don't think he bought it, huh?" Chip said casually, "Oh well. It's no biggie."

"No biggie," I snapped, utterly losing my cool. "Look Chip, I don't know who you are or what planet you came from, but if you ruin my chances of making that all-star team, I swear I'll ... I'll ..." I sputtered as I tried to think of a suitable threat. "I don't know what I'll do, but you'll be sorry. That's for sure."

Chip started laughing. "Calm down, you sound like my mom. Besides, it's just a basketball team. I don't know what the big deal is. Look, I'm hungry. You want to order pizza?"

"What do you mean, 'just a basketball team'?" I echoed, ignoring Chip's pizza offer. "Don't tell me you wouldn't want a spot playing for Coach D. It's, like, the biggest honour in the world."

"Actually, I think that's winning the Nobel Prize," laughed Chip with a big smile. "Look Jeff, I'm sorry. OK? I didn't mean to mess up anything for you. But man, you gotta cut your dosage. I mean, it's only basketball."

Taking a deep breath, I felt a little silly shouting at Chip when he obviously wasn't about to fight back. I just couldn't get a read on this guy. It was like Chip meant well, but he was just really good at messing things up. One thing was clear, though: Chip wasn't excited about playing basketball for the next two weeks.

"Chip," I sighed, my curiosity bubbling over, "why did you come here, anyway? I mean, you're not on some reform-school community-service project or something, are you? Your probation officer isn't forcing you to be here? So what's the deal?"

Chip grinned foolishly and looked pleased that I had asked the question. "I'm here," he said, snatching a brochure from beneath a stack of biking magazines and handing it to me, "for this."

"'The Eastern Canada Mountain Bike Classic'?" I read slowly, staring at the brochure. The cover had a picture of a woman on a bike speeding down a treacherous rocky path so steep that a mountain goat wouldn't venture down it.

"I'm entrant number one-zero-six-eight," said Chip proudly.

"You're racing in this thing?" I exclaimed. I admired his courage, but was now surer than ever that Chip was nuttier than a candy bar.

"Yep. In a couple of days I'll be jamming gears in the biggest race this side of Montreal. As a bonus, all the big names will be there, too," Chip said excitedly, "including him." Chip gestured to a poster of a man on a mountain bike wearing mirrored bug-eyed sunglasses and a green hat flipped backwards.

"Who's he?"

"Flash Freewheeling."

"Flash who?"

"Flash Freewheeling — not his real name of course, but it's easier to get corporate sponsorship if you sound catchy and marketable. He's only the greatest biker on the circuit today and my idol. Totally the best, man."

"Ah-ha. But why are you at basketball camp?" I continued, still not clear on Chip's scheme.

"Well, my folks didn't want me to enter the race. They said it was too dangerous. Big surprise there. My mom thinks the RCMP bike rodeo in the mall parking lot is too dangerous for me. So I said I wanted to come to basketball camp. A couple of weeks away from home, race the coolest race of my life, sprinkle in an autograph from Flash and presto — the best summer vacation I could ask for. I just hope my folks don't figure it out. They'd kill me if they knew."

"Don't worry. I doubt the FBI could figure that plan out."

Chip looked pleased with himself. "Anyway, I'm starved. I'm ordering some 'za." He got up and picked his way through the mess towards the door. "You like mushrooms?"

I nodded slightly as I flopped down on my bed and tried to digest the day's events. Being surrounded by Chip's clutter made my mind even more muddled and I decided to take a walk to clear my head.

The sun was sinking low as I plodded along the street outside of Howe Hall. Turning onto a paved path, I found myself walking along the edge of a soccer field, which bordered on the Dalhousie University campus.

A flash of light suddenly drew my eyes to the middle of the field, where a girl was bent over a strange contraption. Curious, I walked over to get a better look.

The girl was about my age, not too tall, with dark blond hair. Her slight frame was draped with a white lab coat, and she was bent over a weird machine that looked like a large, silver waffle iron hooked up to a laptop computer.

As I got nearer I tried to make a little noise to get the girl's attention, but without any luck. She seemed totally absorbed by the numbers being displayed on the computer screen.

I was almost next to the silver plate when the girl jerked her head up and started shouting. "My sun! You're blocking my sun! Move. Move. Move!"

I didn't know what she was yelling about, but she sure sounded serious so I jumped out of the way and dropped to the ground beside her.

"Sorry," I mumbled, although I didn't have a clue what I was sorry for.

"You really must be more careful when you're around scientific experiments," the girl scolded without looking up.

"Scientific experiments?" I echoed.

"Yes, I'm measuring the potential solar energy generated by the sun in a twelve-hour period," she responded curtly. "By blocking the sun from my solar collector you may have jeopardized the accuracy of my findings."

I wrinkled my brow and guessed that the waffle iron was the solar collector. "Potential energy ..."

"... generated by the sun in one twelve-hour period," the girl repeated. "It's quite simple, really. I hooked the solar cell into my computer, and by running the raw data through a conversion program I should have an answer as soon as the sun goes down."

As I watched the last remaining red rays trickle through the tree tops at the far end of soccer field, I wondered if this girl was playing some sort of joke on me.

"How long have you been sitting here?"

"Twelve hours, of course. I had to make sure nobody disturbed my experiment." She glared at me pointedly.

"Wow," I let out a low whistle. "Good thing nobody wanted to play soccer today."

"Oh, I told them to come back tomorrow," the girl replied.

"Of course." This girl was more into science than David Suzuki. "Can I ask why you're doing this?"

"For fun."

"Right." This activity positively oozed fun. Perhaps only math class could top it on the fun-o-meter.

"There," said the girl, tapping a few last keystrokes and finally looking at me. "I'm Tess Ward, pleased to meet you."

I introduced myself and after a long pause asked a dumb question. "Tess, you're not here for the basketball camp, are you?"

Tess wasn't. It turned out this girl was about three IQ points away from being a certifiable genius. She was attending a special science workshop that brought together supersmart students from all across the province to do fun science things. Fun science stuff, I figured, like staring at a computer screen in the middle of a soccer field for twelve hours. Apparently, as horrified as I was at the idea of doing something as boring as science, Tess felt the same way about basketball.

"Basketball camp, huh?" Tess mused. "I thought I had noticed a lot of neanderthals in Nikes crawling around. So, how do you like it so far?"

I ignored her wisecrack. "It's fun," I replied, overlooking the fact that in just one day I had met my alien roommate, made a bad impression on Coach D. and got severely toasted on the basketball court. "And science camp?" I asked, trying to keep the conversation going.

"It's very intellectually stimulating," Tess said. "Not at all like school, where I'm always being slowed down by average kids," Tess pulled a pack of gum from her pocket and offered me a piece.

I took the gum and popped it in my mouth. "Thanks," I said super-sweetly. I could tell from her tone that I was exactly the type of average kid Tess was referring to.

"It's very refreshing to be in an environment that is so conducive to learning. I just love being surrounded by bright young men and women who can actually discuss scientific problems on the same above-average level as I. In regular school I always feel like an outsider because of my intelligence," she continued.

"Yeah," I said, not quite knowing how to respond. "I know what you mean."

"I doubt that," Tess observed, somehow managing to look down her nose at me, despite the fact that I was taller than her.

There was an awkward pause before she continued. "I'm actually here as a reward for my good grades. My school has a Dalhousie science camp scholarship, which I won because I had the highest average in my grade."

She certainly didn't win because of her stunning personality.

"Anyway," Tess said, concluding the conversation. "I should get back. It's getting chilly and I don't want to catch a cold."

I nodded in agreement, even though I wasn't cold at all. Besides, I wasn't anxious to have a long conversation with Tess. She seemed eager to show me how smart she was while pointing out how dumb I was. What made me mad was that she was very good at it.

"Well, it was nice meeting you," I said finally. "Where are you staying?"

"Howe Hall," Tess replied.

"That's where I'm staying, too."

"Oh, so it's basketball players who are making all that noise below me," Tess said pointedly as she started gathering her various pieces of equipment.

"Too loud for you, huh?"

"Well, not only that, but," Tess paused thoughtfully, "there's a peculiar smell in my room."

"Smell?"

"Yeah," Tess made a face. "It's quite strong. It sort of smells like, well, bicycle grease."

I choked on my gum.

"Isn't that strange?" Tess continued as we walked towards Howe Hall. "I mean who would have a lot of bicycle grease in their room?"

"Some weirdo, probably," I said finally, thinking about my mountain bike fanatic of a roommate. "Yes, definitely some weirdo."

3

Terminal Embarrassment

Heavy-metal music was blasting in room 121. This would have been fine except the digital clock beside my bed told me it was five-thirty in the morning. I groaned. Whoever was blaring music at five-thirty was going to die and I had a feeling that person was Chip Carson.

"Turn it down!" I yelled, stuffing a pillow over my head.

"Sorry, man. My alarm clock is broken. The volume is stuck on high."

"Then perhaps you could turn it *off*," I suggested in a peeved tone of voice.

The music continued.

Angrily, I sat up in bed, fully prepared to throw the alarm clock — and Chip, if possible — through the window. I was shocked by the figure before me.

Crouched over his precious bike, Chip was wearing orange spandex tights, a skin-tight red jersey and beat-up shoulder, elbow and knee pads. On his hands were fingerless gloves with wrist straps wrapped up his forearms. The strange ensemble was capped off by a large mushroom-like helmet with a yellow-tinted visor covering his eyes.

"Oh man, you are too weird," I groaned, giving my roommate a second look. "Please don't tell me you're wearing that to practice this morning."

"I'm afraid I won't be making it to practice today," replied Chip.

"Why? Is the spaceship coming to take you back to Mars?"

"No such luck," said Chip. "I'm going to scout out the course for the bike race next week."

"At five-thirty in the morning?"

"If you don't hit the trails early it's hard to get a good feel for the terrain."

I groaned again.

"Anyway, I didn't mean to wake you up," apologized Chip as he wheeled his bike out the door.

"Blasting your stereo in the middle of the night. Of course you didn't," I yawned. "I guess I'm just a light sleeper."

"Yeah, probably," said Chip, missing my sarcasm completely. "See you later."

**

My lungs were on fire. I felt blood pumping in my ears, and my legs were churning on automatic as I and the rest of the campers ran waves of wind sprints across the Dalhousie gymnasium.

The sprints were fairly simple: run from the baseline to the half-court line and back, run the full length of the gym and back and finally, run to the locker room and collapse from exhaustion. Forget basketball camp, I felt like I was training for a track meet.

"Hustle! Hustle! Hustle!" shouted Coach D., his teeth clenched on a whistle that shrieked every thirty seconds, starting another wave of sprints. "No point playing basketball if you're not even in condition to run the court."

"I'm in condition, all right," groaned Oak, bending over and tugging on his shorts, "critical condition. What is this? Boot camp?"

I tried to laugh, but a stab of pain in my lungs made me cough instead.

The only person not affected by the endless running was Jay Best. In fact, Jay was in such good shape that between sprints, instead of leaning against the wall or tugging on his shorts like the rest of us, he would actually get down on the ground, pump out twenty good push-ups and still beat the pack on the next sprint.

"Who does he think he is, the Energizer Bunny?" panted Oak as we watched Jay spring off the ground and get ready for the next sprint.

"He's nuts," I gasped.

Apparently Coach D. didn't think so. "OK, men, this time when you're finished running, drop and give me twenty, just like Jay!" he called.

A loud groan went up from all the guys. "Make that twenty-five then!" boomed Coach D.

We all groaned again — silently.

After running us for almost half an hour Coach D. mercifully let us get a drink of water.

"Check your team lists and we'll start running some drills when you get back," bellowed Coach D., gesturing to a large chalkboard propped up at the far end of the gym.

With almost two hundred boys, the campers were divided into teams of about fifteen. Each team would run drills in separate areas of the gym and also play together in camp scrimmages against other teams.

Standing in line to get a drink, I gazed up at the enormous Dalplex. With twelve hoops sprouting from the walls, and two glass backboards on the main court, the facility could swallow up all two hundred boys and still look cavernous.

Right now, however, nobody cared about the twelve hoops; with tongues like sandpaper every guy there would rather the Dalplex came equipped with twelve drinking fountains, instead.

"Hey, Camel Boy! Save some for the rest of us, huh?" Oak bellowed as a guy took a particularly long drink at the fountain.

"So, I think we're all on the same team," observed Scott as he tried to untangle the mass of jewellery hanging from his neck.

"That's good. If we have a good team, Coach D. will probably look at us a little more and that means we have a better chance of making the all-star squad," added Oak.

Glad I wasn't the only one constantly thinking about the juvenile all-star team, I nodded absently as the drinking-fountain line shuffled forward. Glancing at the large chalkboard, I made a face when I noticed that super-athlete Jay Best was also on my team.

"So we have drills for two hours, then lunch," chattered Scott, not noticing he was now at the head of the line. "After lunch it's our first scrimmage and we have to be here at —"

"Yeah, thanks for the news bulletin but we all have a schedule," interrupted Oak, pointing at the drinking fountain. "Now drink."

"Oh, whoops." Scott bent over and started gulping the fountain water.

"So what do you think so far?" Oak asked, catching me looking around.

"Pretty cool. How about you?"

"It's great. We've been here every summer for three years, now. Me and Scotty both. This camp is the best. Drink up, would ya!" He slapped his friend on the hip while he was drinking. "Yeah," Oak continued, turning back to me, "we do practices in the morning and halfway through the afternoon

and then we have scrimmages before supper and in the evening. The team with the best record at the end gets T-shirts,
but that's not the big prize."

"That's being picked for the all-star team," gulped Scott
in between drinks of water.

"Shut up and drink!" boomed Oak.

"Everyone wants to make the all-star team. I made it last
year and it was seriously the best time of my life," Oak turned
back towards the fountain. "Scotty, buddy, hurry up would
ya? I'm dying of thirst back here!"

Scott waved Oak off and kept drinking.

"The coach of our scrimmage team is Donovan. He's
twenty years old and plays for the Dalhousie varsity team.
He's pretty cool. We've got some good players on our team,
and from what I've seen, you keep nailing those jumpers and
you'll be in the running for a spot on the all-star team. C'mon
Scotty, let me get a drink!"

Scott made a rude gesture behind his back at Oak.

"That's it," yelled Oak, grabbing Scott's baggy silk shorts
and hauling them down to the boy's ankles.

"Hey," screamed Scott, jerking his head up too quickly
and crowning himself on the metal casing of the fountain.
"Ow! Ow! Ow!" Shorts still around his ankles, Scott started
dancing around in pain, trying to rub his bruised head with
one hand and trying to pull up his shorts with the other. He
couldn't quite manage to do either, but he sure looked funny.

"Oh, have we finished our little drink?" asked Oak
sweetly, as he moved to the fountain.

Everybody in line howled as Scott booted Oak in the
behind and then got chased around the gym. I laughed too. I
tried to forget about how lousy my first day had been. There
were some cool guys here, and I decided I should take it easy
and try to have a good time. Being away from school and

away from Sharon and my dad was beginning to make me feel very relaxed and grown up.

Oak and Scott were still chasing each other and play-fighting when Coach D. blew the whistle for us to split up into our teams.

Oak was right when he said our scrimmage-team coach was cool. Donovan was about six foot four and was always cracking jokes and clowning around with us. He also knew basketball. This morning we were doing layup drills.

Donovan had us line up thirty feet away from the hoop in two lines at either side of the basket. One line was given a couple of balls, and as one guy ran in to do a layup, the guy at the front of the other line would run in and get his rebound and go to the end of the layup line. It was a simple drill and I had done it about a thousand times before, so I was pretty relaxed and playing well. About as well as Jay Best, I figured. And I would know, too, because when I didn't have the ball my eyes were fixed on him, comparing my performance with his.

Scrimmage-team coaches like Donovan would set the drills in motion, and then Coach D. would make his way around and look at each squad individually. When Coach D. was nearby, everyone concentrated a little more on his game.

We were doing a tricky layup and passing drill when Coach D. wandered over to our corner of the gym for a second time. Showing him my stuff, I raced in for a layup only to be blinded by a flash of light coming from under the hoop.

Clang! I banged my layup off the underside of the rim. It wasn't until I heard a familiar voice that I realized what had happened.

"Nice try, honey," shouted Sharon from under the basket. "Next time, look my way," she called waving her camera. My rebound was bouncing right to her, and Sharon bent over and picked up the basketball.

Suffering from a terminal case of embarrassment, I turned away just in time to see Coach D. shake his head and walk off.

"Hey Jeff, you know that lady?" called Donovan, jogging towards me.

"Um yeah, she's my stepmom," I said quietly.

"Your stepma, huh?" boomed Donovan, just loud enough for the entire gym to hear. "Well, you think you can ask her to give us the ball back so we can keep practising?"

Sheepishly, I hustled over to Sharon, feeling every eye in the gym burning into my back.

"Hi, darling," cried Sharon, trying to give me a peck on the cheek.

"Are you nuts?" I growled, snatching the ball from her and throwing it back into play. "What are you doing here?"

"My meetings broke off for a few hours, so I thought I'd come and see how you were making out."

"I was making out fine before you showed up." I was no longer embarrassed, now I was just mad.

"Did I make you nervous, honey?" she soothed, touching my arm. "I noticed you missed that shot."

"I missed because you flashed that camera in my face," I cried, bristling at her touch.

"Oh, I thought it would be cute to get some pictures of you playing."

Suddenly I wished I was in science camp with Tess instead of looking like a wimp in front of a gym full of guys.

"I got to go," I said. "Please don't show up at practice again, Sharon. You really shouldn't be here."

"I'm sorry, dear," Sharon called, putting the camera in her purse. "I just wanted to see how you were doing."

"See ya," I said briskly as I jogged back to my team.

"Hey Lang," called Oak as I rejoined the drill. "Next time get her to bring some milk and cookies, would ya?"

All the guys cracked up and I felt like a total dweeb. Thanks a lot, Sharon.

My feelings of embarrassment continued as Donovan called out the next drill. It was another layup drill, but now we had to make the layup while being guarded by a defender. As my rotten luck would have it I ended up guarding Jay. It was bad enough guarding him when my mind was on the game, but the way I was feeling now, Jay took me to school faster than my bus driver.

"C'mon Lang, move those feet," cried Donovan as Jay scooted by me for another layup. "What are you wearing, lead sneakers?"

The torture finally ended when Coach D. blew his whistle and called all the campers together.

"Good work, men," he said. He was the only coach I ever had who talked in a normal voice in a gym and still got everyone's attention. "I see that we have a lot of work to do over the next two weeks, but I also see we have some great talent to work with." I noticed that Coach D. was staring right at Jay while he said that.

"One other thing, men," he continued. "We're missing a camper."

I felt a hot feeling rush over me as I thought about my crazy roommate out ploughing through the woods somewhere. The feeling lasted only a second, however. Why should I care if Coach D. nailed Chip for skipping practice? It didn't have anything to do with me.

"Jeff Lang, are you here?" Coach D. said, as if he could read my mind.

"Right here, sir," I piped up. Some of the guys started whispering and snickering.

"Where's your roommate, Chip Carson, son?"

Why is he asking me, I wondered. I'm his roommate, not his mother. "I don't know, Coach," I answered, hoping that would be it.

"What do you mean, you don't know?" Coach D. repeated. "I put a strong emphasis on teamwork around here. The whole camp is a team, the scrimmage squads are a team, and I'm looking for special players for my all-star team. Each pair of roommates is supposed to act like a team. Now Lang, it looks like you and your roommate let your teammates down." Coach D. took a moment to let his words sink in, and believe me, they were sinking like the Titanic in my stomach. "That's all, men. See you tomorrow."

The rest of the boys drifted out of the gym as I stood there staring at my shoes.

I couldn't believe I got chewed out for not knowing where Chip Carson was. What did Coach D. want? Was I supposed to chain Chip to my wrist and drag him around wherever I went? I shuddered at the thought.

4

What a Gas

Trudging back to Howe Hall I decided I had seen better days. The only consolation was that so many bad things had happened, I couldn't decide which was the worst. It was probably a toss-up between Sharon babying me in front of two hundred guys and Coach D. yelling at me for not knowing where Chip was. Jay Best making me look like a chump on the court was pretty bad too, but I was getting used to that.

When I reached room 121 all I wanted to do was kick off my sweaty sneakers and sleep for the rest of the week. Much to my dismay the door to the room was locked.

"Perfect," I grumbled. "Chip? You in there?" I called, banging the door. "Open up, would you!"

After a long pause I concluded that the wheeled weirdo was still out wandering in the woods.

"Hey, you locked out?" came a voice down the hall.

I turned and saw Jay Best sauntering my way. In the dim lighting of the hallway I half hoped he wouldn't notice me rolling my eyes.

"You locked out?" Jay repeated his question.

"Yeah," I replied, "my roommate's got the key."

"Where's your roommate?"

I thought about the question carefully. "In the woods somewhere between here and New Brunswick," I answered quite truthfully.

"Right," he replied, unfazed by the bizarre answer. "Look, it stinks to be locked out here in the hall. Why don't you hang out in my room until he gets back?"

"Sure, sounds good," I mumbled, being as honest as a used-car salesman.

"Cool," said Jay, leading me down the hall towards his own room.

As Jay opened the door, I was immediately struck by the extreme cleanliness of the room. Of course, after Chip's mess a landfill site would seem orderly.

"Have a seat," offered Jay, pointing to a chair propped up beside the desk. I was surprised at how comfortable the chair was. I hadn't actually sat in the chair in my own room because it was currently being used to hold the last thirty-six issues of *Mountain Biking Weekly.*

Looking around, I tried to adjust to being in a dorm room where I could actually see the carpet. It was eerie. Jay's room was a notch above regular cleanliness. It was almost hospital-clean.

Both single beds were neatly made and there were two duffle bags tidily stowed underneath the desk. The only thing out of order was a closet door slightly ajar. I winced as I noticed about twelve freshly pressed white T-shirts hanging in a row, all exactly the same as the one Jay was currently wearing.

"You want some mineral water?" Jay offered, unzipping the gym bag hanging from his shoulder and taking out two plastic water bottles. "I'm afraid it's all I have. I only drink water or low-fat milk."

"Really? Me too," I joked. Jay laughed awkwardly as he neatly flipped one of the bottles my way. Unfortunately, it slipped through my hands, clunked loudly onto the floor and rolled under the bed.

"Whoops, bad throw," commented Jay, cracking his own bottle and taking a long drink.

I smiled weakly, as I got on all fours and peered under Jay's bed. I quickly grabbed the bottle and scrambled to my feet. I was no longer thristy, just embarrassed.

"Oh, give me a second," mumbled Jay as he started scratching in a little black book.

"Writing down your girlfriend's phone number?" I asked, trying to make another joke.

"Actually, I'm writing down some personal statistics," replied Jay seriously.

"Statistics?" I repeated, setting my bottled water down on Jay's desk and taking a closer look.

"Yes, you know, rebounds, foul shots, left-handed layups, how many shots I take, how many I make. That sort of thing." Jay opened the book so I could see a complex chart full of different basketball activities followed by dates and numbers.

"You remember all the things that happen in practice?" I asked, unable to believe what I was seeing.

"Oh no, these are extra drills I do on my own time. I do them in the summer to get ready for next season. I also graph them on a computer so I can see how much better I'm getting." Jay laid the notebook on the desk.

"Wow." I was impressed. Frightened, but impressed. "You mind if I look at that?"

"Go ahead," said Jay, unlacing his sneakers and carefully placing them side by side on the floor of his closet.

I reached out to pick up Jay's book, accidentally knocking over my bottle of water with my elbow.

"Whoops," I cried, trying to grab the bottle as a wave of water splashed onto Jay's precious practice log.

"My book," Jay called, leaping across the room, scooping up his book and righting the bottle in one smooth motion.

"Sorry about that," I said sheepishly.

Jay was tight-lipped as he tried to dry his book. "No problem."

We sat in awkward silence for a moment. I wasn't exactly a master of small talk at the best of times, and after slopping water across Jay's book I was really feeling like a king-sized dork.

"So what do you think of the camp so far?" Jay finally asked, giving me a thin smile and placing his black book back inside his gym bag.

"It's good," I replied, trying desperately to think of something to keep the conversation going. Finally I came up with, "How about you?" Brilliant.

"You know, same old thing. I've been here twice before. It's fun and Coach D. is great. I really like playing for him, and the juvenile all-star team is a lot of fun at the end of camp."

I pretended to be surprised. "Oh, you made that team before, huh?"

Jay was cooler than an air-conditioned igloo. "Yeah, twice," he replied, setting down his bottle of water and peeling off his sweaty white T-shirt. I couldn't help noticing that Jay had muscles in places where I didn't even have places yet.

Jay went to the closet and tugged a fresh white T-shirt over his head. "But there's a lot of good players here this year," Jay added. "It might be tough to make the cut. I'm hoping but I don't know ..."

Yeah right, I thought, and Patrick Ewing doesn't know if he's going to make the Knicks this year.

"So what's it like to play for Coach D.?" I had to ask. I'd been wondering about it since I signed up for the camp.

"Well, he's a tough coach and he's really intense during games. In a time-out last year he was yelling at us so hard his dentures flew out. He just bent over, scooped them up, popped them back in his mouth and kept yelling like nothing had even happened. No one even dared smile and it was probably the funniest thing I ever saw."

I laughed in spite of myself.

"And one time on the way to a game, the bus driver took a wrong turn and Coach D. got so mad he kicked the driver off the bus and drove the rest of the way himself."

"No way."

"Yeah, you don't want to mess with Coach D. when he's mad. Then there was this other time —"

Jay's story was interrupted by a strange noise coming down the hall. It was a high-pitched whizzing sound accompanied by a loud wail.

Jay and I looked out the doorway in time to see a multicoloured blur zip by, followed a few seconds later by a loud crash coming from down the hall.

"What was that?" exclaimed Jay, sounding less than cool for the first time since I met him.

"That would be my roommate," I sighed, getting up and pitching my empty bottle in the blue box under the desk. "Thanks for the water."

"No problem. You can hang here for a while if you want. Your roommate seems a little ... you know ..." Jay made little crazy circles by his ear.

"No thanks. I'll see you at practice." For the first time I was almost glad to see Chip.

Once I'd returned to my room that gladness disintegrated pretty fast. After the sterile confines of Jay's room, being back in my pig sty was a little jarring, never mind the fact that a mud-caked mountain bike was blocking the doorway. From the bike a trail of mud led to a mud-caked Chip, still in his mountain-bike gear, collapsed on a now mud-caked bed. There were two beds in the room. Chip had chosen to collapse on mine. Perfect.

Spotting me standing in the doorway, Chip sprang to life.

"What a rush, man," he cried, sitting up on the edge of my bed. "That was the best trail I ever rode in my life."

"Is there any of it left in the woods, or did you bring it all back to our room?" I inquired dryly.

"Yeah, I guess it is a little muddy," said Chip, looking around at the mainly brown surroundings.

That's an understatement, I thought, any remaining gladness to see Chip rapidly draining away. "You know, Chip, I really can't believe you ..." I said, losing my temper and getting ready to lay into my obnoxious roommate who suddenly seemed very capable of turning my basketball paradise into something more irritating than chafing underwear, "... do you really think that you have the right to come in here and—"

I stopped short and wrinkled my nose as I caught a whiff of the foulest odour I had ever smelled. "Is that you?" I coughed. "'Cause if it is you better get to the bathroom — or the hospital!"

"It's not me, man," replied Chip, covering his nose and rapidly fanning his hand in front of his face. "But whatever it is it's pretty rank."

He wasn't kidding. Coughing and gagging, we were steadily overcome by a smell worse than skunk, rotten eggs and bad foot odour all put together.

Barely able to see through my watering eyes, I glanced upwards only to discover a fine pinkish gas seeping through the air vent in the ceiling.

"Look!" I exclaimed. "Somebody upstairs set off a stink bomb in the air vent."

Chip and I bolted from our room and ran up a nearby stairwell to investigate the source of the smell.

No sooner had we turned into the upstairs hallway than we saw billows of the pink gas spewing from an open doorway and a choking Tess Ward slumped against the wall.

Rushing to her aid, I soon realized that Tess wasn't choking — she was laughing.

"I did it!" she cried as I kneeled down to see if she was all right.

"It's OK, the smell will go away soon."

"No, you don't understand," replied Tess, losing her smile and giving Chip and me a sharp look. "I did it. I successfully combined hydrogen chloride with barium hydroxide! My lab teacher said you couldn't do it!"

"You sure he didn't say you shouldn't do it," piped up Chip, covering his nose and mouth with his shirt. "This place smells pretty gross!"

"It'll air out soon," said Tess. For someone who was bothered by the smell of bicycle grease coming from one floor below, she sure didn't seem to mind the rancid stench that she had created. "Besides, it's a small price to pay for science."

"Does that price include dry cleaning? I'll never wash this stink out of my clothes," Chip replied.

Tess thrust out her chin defiantly. "Small minds have always tried to prevent advancements in science," she said tersely.

"And why exactly were you advancing science in your room?" Chip replied. "Don't they have a nerd gym or something for you to play in?"

"It's called a laboratory," Tess snapped, "and it's closed. Besides, our instructor said we could perform minor experiments in our room."

I didn't think creating toxic gas was a minor experiment and I was about to say so when some people charged out of their rooms to investigate the strange odour. In the lead was a small man wearing a white lab coat and carrying a clipboard. He looked pretty brainy and he certainly wasn't a basketball coach.

"Good work, Tess!" the man exclaimed as he got nearer.

"Yeah, good work," muttered Chip under his breath. "You managed to stink the place out."

"I see you performed the experiment I told you about," the man continued. "Smells like you used a little too much zinc oxide in your stabilizing solution, though," the man laughed.

"Maybe a little," Tess giggled. A few of the other science campers laughed too and suddenly Chip and I felt very out of place.

"Oh well," the man continued, "the smell will go away in a few days. In the meantime you probably shouldn't stay in that room."

"But all my stuff ..." Tess protested.

"No buts," the man smiled and flipped through a stack of papers on his clipboard. "Ah, here we go," he said finally. "We can move you downstairs to room 120."

I winced. Tess was going to move into the room across the hall from me. It was bad enough that I was living with one weirdo, I certainly didn't want another one across the hall ... even if it was for the advancement of science.

5

Love Is in the Air?

The next few days passed uneventfully. Chip actually showed up to a couple of practices and I tried — and usually failed — to get Coach D. to notice me. I was finding out a lot about the Dalhousie basketball camp, mainly that most of the other players there were older, bigger and better than me. Don't get me wrong, it's not like I was getting embarrassed on the court — except maybe when I had to guard Jay Best — it was just that I couldn't turn any heads. Especially not Coach D.'s. Still, I was confident I could turn things around and crack the line-up of the all-star team. Starting today I had vowed to play harder than ever.

That morning the ill-timed and very loud malfunction of Chip's alarm clock caused Chip and me to arrive early for practice. I was happy to be shooting around in the nearly empty Dalplex, but my sleepy-eyed roommate was not so pleased.

"I cannot believe we're here early," he yawned.

"Well if your alarm hadn't gone nuts at six we wouldn't be," I countered, pretending to be more upset about the early hour than I actually was. In fact, I was already awake when the clock went off and now I was anxious to hit the hardwood.

"Well, I'm getting a new alarm clock then," Chip muttered grumpily. "The less time I have to spend in the gym the better. I'm going to rest until practice begins."

With that, Chip headed to the far bleachers and sunk low in the last row.

Once Chip had trudged off, I turned my attention to a game of three-on-three that some other guys were playing on a nearby court. "I got game!" I called, letting them know that I wanted to play.

Scuffing my sneakers on the hardwood floor I tried to forget about the rough start to my camping career.

Although organized ball with coaches and refs and all that was OK, I really thrived on pick-up basketball. There was nothing quite like being in a near-empty gym, playing no-blood-no-foul-straight-up-in-your-face-tough-defence-trash-talking-taking-it-to-the-hole-get-out-of-my-way hoops to re-mind me how much I loved the game.

Out on the court, a heavyset guy with long hair tied back in a pony-tail made a tricky fall-away jumper. "That's seven. Take a seat, guys," he said to the losing team. "Who's next?"

"I'm up," I called, rushing onto the floor, ready to play.

"You got a team or are you going to take us on yourself?" The guy with the pony-tail was only a little older and taller than me but he looked more muscular. He had a mean face and a gold earring in his left ear. The boy's teammates laughed at his joke and I felt hot with embarrassment.

Searching for teammates, I wasn't surprised to see Jay Best drift into the gym to do some extra drills before morning practice. Seeing a game just about to start, Jay eagerly agreed to be on my team.

"You don't count too good, do you?" ribbed the tough guy impatiently. "You still need another player, stupid."

This guy thought he was hot stuff, but he had me. I glared at him and looked around helplessly. There wasn't another teammate in sight.

"Hey, how about that guy?" Jay suggested, pointing to Chip reclining on the bleachers.

Honestly, I would rather play two-on-three than ask Chip to play, but the team on the court had their arms crossed and were glaring with impatience.

"Well, go get him," sneered the pony-tail guy.

Seeing there was no other option, I grimaced and trotted over to collect my roommate.

"Hey Chip!" I called. There was no response. "Chip!"

With large headphones sprouting from his ears, Chip was grooving to his tunes, eyes closed, blissfully unaware of everything around him. As I got closer I could hear Chip singing.

"Oh baby, baby, take a look at me baby, I wanna be your man, baby, baby, oh baby," Chip droned tunelessly.

I booted Chip in the foot.

"Hey! What's up, Jeff?" Chip shouted, finally noticing me.

"Do you want to play three-on-three?" I asked, pointing at the guys waiting on the court.

"What's that? I can't hear you," replied Chip, pointing at the large headphones on his ears, but not taking them off.

"Come on," I shouted, snatching Chip's portable CD player and turning it off. "We need a third player. You want in?"

"It's very tempting," he said finally, pretending to think over the proposition, "but I'm afraid I'll have to decline."

"Come on, Chip," I pleaded.

"No thanks." Chip reached for the "on" button on his CD player.

I played my last card. "Please Chip, would you do it for me? As a favour to your roommate?"

Chip gave me an odd look, but finally agreed.

At last ready to start, I had a chance to check out the competition.

Besides the pony-tail guy, there was a slender kid dressed entirely in a replica Toronto Raptors uniform and a short chunky boy with a round face and droopy red shorts.

"Chip, you guard the guy in the red shorts," I instructed, huddling up with my teammates and collecting my cool. "Jay, how about you take Damon Stoudamire over there. I'll take the tough guy with the pretty hair."

Taking the check at the top of the key, the pony-tail guy handed me the ball with mock politeness. "After making us wait so long, I hope you guys are good," he growled.

"The way you play, Goldie Locks, you better hope we're not, or else you're going to lose," I growled back. Off the court, I was hardly a loudmouth, but on the court it was a different story. I wasn't shy about lipping off and talking a little trash. Besides, this guy had tried to make me look bad.

The long-haired guy was good and he knew it, but I was determined to take it to him. It's never a good idea to let your emotions take over on the court, but the way this clown strutted around just made me want to show him up.

Right off the check, I made a quick jab fake and burned by him. Trying to stop the easy layup, the guy in the Raptor uniform stepped into the lane and tried to slow me down. That left Jay sitting all by himself under the basket. Seeing the open man, I dropped a neat little bounce pass to Jay, who notched the easy bucket.

"Great pass, Jeff!" Jay cried.

"One nothing," I called out, slapping five with Jay. Although playing against him drove me crazy, it was nice to know at least one of my teammates was good.

"I know the score," grunted the thick guy with the pony-tail. "I can count, you know."

"But probably not higher than ten, right?" I shot back. Jay cracked a small smile and checked the ball at the top of the circle.

I cut through the key and took a pass from Jay on the left side of the hoop. Looking over the situation, I saw Chip brushing by his man and standing open near the basket calling for the ball. Shaking him off I tried to make a pass back to Jay, but the pass was too high and was picked off by Jay's defender.

"Nice play, Ahmed!" cried the pony-tail guy, clapping at my mistake.

"Hey Jeff," cried Chip. "What's up with that? I was open like a 7-Eleven store down there! Gimme the rock."

I rolled my eyes and waved off Chip's complaint. I was playing to win and I figured Chip couldn't throw a rock in the ocean, let alone the ball in the hoop.

Clearing the ball, Ahmed fired it over to the short guy in the red shorts. Chip rushed out to play defence as his man made a move to go to the hoop. I was a little shocked to see Chip's muscular legs pumping up and down as he shuffled quickly towards the baseline, cutting off his man. Even though he didn't have a lane, the chunky boy wouldn't pass off and Chip made the steal and scampered to clear the ball.

"Good job!" cried Jay.

But Chip wasn't finished. Hovering close to the ground, he threaded the ball between his legs and weaved his way through traffic towards the hoop. Zipping by two defenders, Chip took off for a layup right in the face of the bulky pony-tail guy. Only instead of going right at him, Chip extended his body and kissed the ball high off the backboard on the other side of the bucket.

My jaw dropped. I couldn't believe that my bike-crazy roommate had just pulled off such a tough reverse layup.

Chip just jogged back to the top of the key and took the check.

With a few more quick scores my team had taken a five-to-two lead. The guy with the pony-tail didn't like this one bit, but I was loving it.

"Nice lid, hot-stuff," I ribbed as the thick boy tried to post me up. "Where do you get it cut? The Play-Doh Mop Shop?" The pony-tail guy just grunted and tried to shove me out of the way.

Our team was passing the ball around well and I could feel myself getting into a rhythm. Chip was surprisingly good for someone who complained about having to play, and Jay was much more fun to play with than against.

Just before I popped in a ten-foot jumper to win the game, I noticed that Coach D. was watching from the far sidelines. I didn't know how long he had been there, but he was bent over tugging on his black gym pants and staring at us intently. I was glad that I had just scored the winning hoop, because knowing that Coach D. was watching made me feel all tight inside.

After the game — and after the guy with the long hair called me something that would have probably got him grounded had his mother heard him — I was waiting by the drinking fountain with Chip when Coach D. walked over.

I didn't know what to expect. The last time Coach D. had talked to me he had given me a real earful. I was a little nervous at what he was going to say to me. Nervous, but excited, too.

"Nice playing out there, boys," he said, clapping Chip and me on the shoulder. "Good shooting and good passing. That's the type of teamwork I like to see. Keep it up." He then patted my shoulder once more, nodded his head and walked away.

"Did you hear that?" I cried to Chip. "Coach D. noticed us! Coach D. noticed me!"

"That guy smells like a Ben Gay factory," replied Chip, wrinkling up his nose and looking bored.

I was not about to let Chip ruin this moment. Even though the Coach had only said a couple of sentences I couldn't have been happier if the man had told me I was just drafted by the Bulls! I was still grinning like an idiot when Coach D. drifted by once again.

"One thing though, son," he said, shaking his head. "You shouldn't talk so much trash out there. It's not good sportsmanship. Just look at Jay Best. He's a good solid player, but he's also a good sport. That's important." Coach D. patted my shoulder once more and walked away.

I felt my stomach sink into my shoes. It took me five days to get Coach D. to notice me and it took him five seconds to burst my bubble. I looked at Chip and shook my head miserably. Chip just rolled his eyes.

"Definitely too much Ben Gay," he said, waving his hand in front of his face to clear the air.

I grinned and Chip and I both started laughing. I felt a little better. I decided I shouldn't be so hard on myself. After all, a compliment from the coach shouldn't be taken lightly. Replaying his positive comments through my head a few more times, I was soon on top of the world again.

That feeling stayed with me all through practice and the scrimmages, and I have to admit it was a great day. I just couldn't miss. I was running drills flawlessly and hitting shots in games that I usually couldn't make in a game of H-O-R-S-E. It wasn't my shoes, but I felt like I was running on air. I guess you could say I was in the zone.

Not only was I playing well, but Coach D. seemed to be always looking at me and yelling "good hustle" or "way to go" whenever I made a play.

I had always known I had what it took to impress Coach D., now I was doing it. But still, it was hard to believe.

Looking back, I guess I shouldn't have believed it.

***

"This is too much!" I cried as Chip and I were walking back to Howe Hall. "I can't believe Jay Best won Camper of the Day!"

"Big deal," yawned Chip. "Let him have the stinking T-shirt. It's not like he won an Academy Award or something."

"It's not the T-shirt, Chip," I fumed. "It's the fact that I couldn't have played better today. I did everything the best I could possibly do it — better even — and that guy still smoked me."

Once we got to Howe Hall, I didn't feel like sitting in our dorm room. So instead I went to blow off some steam on the court behind the building. To my surprise, Chip came with me.

"He really eats you up inside, doesn't he?" Chip asked, taking a seat on the grass at the edge of the court. "That Jay guy."

"Only because he's taller than me, faster than me, a better shooter than me, stronger than me and will make Coach D.'s all-star squad before me. Other than that, he doesn't bother me at all."

"So you're jealous of him?"

"No, not jealous," I spat. "Well, OK, maybe a little, but it burns me because he's just too perfect. Perfect looking, perfect clothes, perfect player. He just makes me want to perfectly puke."

"You're right," agreed Chip. "The guy is definitely a little hard to stomach."

"I'll say. Jay Best could fall into a tub of horse manure and with his luck he'd find a diamond ring in it."

I was about to take another jump shot, when four kids wearing white science coats and waving various pieces of science equipment came storming onto the court.

"Excuse us, science students coming through!" called Tess Ward, who, not surprisingly, was leading the invasion. I grimaced. Since she had moved across the hall from us I had managed to avoid Tess.

"Tess! What do you think you're doing?" I called, annoyed to be forced off the court by a bunch of science fanatics.

"We're plotting vector coordinates. This space happens to be the resultant vector in one of our calculations."

"Congratulations, now what are you doing? Having a parade because someone finished a math problem?"

"No," Tess said, adopting an even more superior tone of voice than usual. "Now we have to do some calculations at this point to check our work."

"Well, see if you can understand this equation," I said, angry that Tess thought she could just march onto the basketball court and make me leave. "One basketball hoop plus one guy with a basketball equals: I'm shooting hoops here, so get off the court!"

"All I see is another dumb jock playing a dumb game," retorted Tess. "Now, if you'd kindly move out of the way, we have some important measurements to do here."

"No, I will not kindly move out of the way," I hollered. "I was here first, so why don't you and your psycho friends in the white coats go and nerd out somewhere else."

"We'll only be a second. I'd explain to you exactly why we have to be right on the court, but you just wouldn't understand it."

"I'm not stupid, you know."

Tess raised her eyebrows and looked at me sceptically. "Of course not, you're a regular genius," she chided, giving her friends a sly look. "Wait. Can the average basketball player even spell 'genius'?" Her friends laughed at her nasty comment.

"Go snort dirt," I shot back. It wasn't a very subtle comeback, but it got my point across. "Just because I play basketball doesn't mean I'm stupid."

"And just because I'm smart doesn't mean that I can't play basketball," retorted Tess.

Now she had gone too far. I smiled; I knew I had her.

"Oh yeah?" I said, spitting on the ground and shoving the ball into Tess's arms. "Prove it. Do or die. Sink a shot from the spit mark and I'll leave. Miss, you guys go play science somewhere else."

I shot a smile at Chip, who was still quietly watching from the grass.

"Deal," said Tess, much too quickly for my liking. The small girl gripped the ball tightly and stared hard at the hoop. "OK. Angle of trajectory: seventy-eight degrees," she mused, bouncing the ball clumsily. "Maximum flight path: approximately five point seven metres. Wind factor: about three knots southeast." Completing her bizarre calculations, Tess bounced the ball twice more and then heaved it skyward with an underhand granny shot. The ball stayed in the air for what seemed like an hour. Finally it came down. *Swish!* I couldn't believe it.

Tess and her friends started cheering and I had no choice but to slink off the court in defeat.

"Try and be quick, OK?" I said, choking on my pride, and sitting down heavily beside Chip on the grass next to the court.

"Man, you got hosed big-time," my roommate said, trying not to laugh.

"Shut up, Chip," I growled. I wasn't in the mood. I tried to wait patiently while Tess and her science gang took measurements and made notes on the court, but it was too painful to watch.

"I can't stand this," I said. "I'm going inside for a minute."

Chip, who was half dozing, nodded absently as I got up and stalked away from the court. As I walked off I snuck a peek at Tess. I couldn't tell if she was making a face at me or just squinting into the sun, but I made a face back just to be on the safe side.

Back inside the foyer of Howe Hall I paced back and forth and tried to calm down. I just couldn't believe that Tess had hit that shot. I mean, what kind of a fluke was that? I was still shaking my head in disbelief when Jay Best sauntered over to me with a strange look on his face.

"What's going on, Jeff?"

"Nothing. Why?" I asked suspiciously. Jay Best and I had hadn't talked much since that day I slopped mineral water all over his room, and I wondered why he was going out of his way to make conversation with me now.

"No reason," Jay shrugged. "Say, Jeff, do you know that girl out there?"

"What girl?" I said shortly. When I was in a good mood I found it hard to talk to Jay, and right now, I was not in a good mood.

"That girl you were playing basketball with."

Perfect, I thought, not only did Tess humiliate me in front of all her friends and my roommate, but apparently everyone at the camp had witnessed my embarrassment.

"The girl I was playing basketball with …?" I said vaguely. Playing dumb was my only hope, I figured.

"Yeah. The one with the blond hair. I was just hoping you knew her because—" Jay stopped short. "Aww, never mind. I'll see you later."

"Oh, *that* girl," I said finally. "Yeah, I know her."

Jay melted. "You do?" I wasn't completely sure, but it looked like Jay Best, super-athlete and perfect-guy *extraordinaire* had the hots for Tess. Perhaps this situation wasn't so bad after all.

"Yeah, we met the first day and we talk quite a bit," I continued, enjoying the look on Jay's face.

"Well, maybe you ... could you ... um ... you know ... introduce me?" Jay said awkwardly, trying to regain his composure.

"Introduce you?" I choked. Good job, Lang, way to stick your foot in it. I could have just played it cool, but no, I had to go and get Jay all excited and now I was caught. "Oh, I don't think that would be a good idea," I said, shaking my head.

"Why not?" Jay looked hurt.

"Oh, because," my mind was racing, "she'd probably be more impressed if you introduced yourself."

Jay grinned. I didn't think it was possible for a guy like him to look goofy, but he did. "Oh, I couldn't do that," he said sheepishly.

"Sure you can," I said mischievously. "I heard she really likes jocks."

"Really," Jay replied, wide-eyed.

"Yeah. But Jay, if you talk to her, don't let her know I told you. She probably wouldn't like you talking about her behind her back."

Jay gave me a thumbs up. "Thanks, Jeff."

I could barely swallow my smile until I got back outside. By the time I reached the court I was laughing my head off.

"Wow, rapid mood change or what," observed Chip.

"You'll never believe what I just found out," I said.

"How they get the caramel inside the Caramilk bar?" Chip offered.

Letting Chip's wisecrack slide, I told him about Jay's crush on Tess. Chip was stunned. "That's just bizarre, man," was all he could say.

As Tess and her science friends departed, Chip and I laughed a bit more about the lovestruck Jay.

I continued to play ball and Chip continued to laze in the grass as the warm summer sun was sinking over the soccer field. Still with a hot hand, I couldn't get over how well I was shooting the ball. From the baseline or at the top of the key, it just didn't matter; every flick of my wrist was met with a swish as the ball ripped through the net. When you're as hot as I was there's only one thing that you want — someone to play against.

"Hey Chip, wanna play some one-on-one?"

Chip raised an eyebrow and wiped a stray strand of red hair from his face. "You gotta be joking," he laughed.

"Come on," I replied, "just a quick game to eleven."

"No thanks," Chip declined.

"Why, are you scared I'll beat you?" I goaded.

"No. I know you'll beat me," replied Chip nonchalantly.

"A quick game to seven, then?" I countered.

"I will not play you to eleven, I will not play a game to seven. I will not play you on a boat, I will not play you with a goat," rhymed Chip, rolling back on the grass and looking happy with his Dr. Seuss-like rhyme.

"Please?"

"No. Now stop it,"

"Don't be such a baby. Just one game," I pleaded, burying a jump shot from the far corner.

"Nope," Chip replied.

"Please, as a favour for your roommate?"

Chip wasn't buying it. "Not this time, thanks."

"Come on," I cried. I was really revved up to play.

"No," shouted Chip, finally losing it. "No. Can't you understand that? I don't like playing on a team. I don't like playing one-on-one. In fact, I don't like playing basketball period! I'm here to race my bike and get some time away from my freaky parental units. That's it. So back off, OK." And with that Chip got up and stormed off.

I took another shot from the top of the foul circle. It clanged badly off the back of the rim. I had been told.

***

When I got back to our room Chip had his head submerged in a back issue of *Mountain Biking Weekly* and there was half a pizza on my bed.

"Sorry, I kinda freaked out there, man," Chip mumbled, barely looking up from his magazine. "I just get a little tense about this whole competitive sports thing. Anyway, have some pizza."

"Hey, mushroom, pineapple, hot peppers and onions, great," I took a bite of the foul combination and did my best not to gag. "This hits the spot," I lied, gingerly nibbling on Chip's peace offering. "Thanks, Chip."

"No problem. The 'za place was having a contest. Order a combination they've never heard of and they'll name it after you," Chip said, putting down the magazine and smiling broadly. "So the next time you order from Vinny's just ask for a fifteen-inch Chip Carson special."

Chip started laughing and so did I. Chip was too much. Besides, if I laughed a lot I didn't have to eat so much.

I lay down on my bed and looked over the schedule for the next day's practice. "Looks like tomorrow we spend about half the day learning how to rebound," I observed.

"Hmmm, too bad I'll have to miss that," replied Chip with mock sadness. "I'll be a little busy."

"Doing what?"

"Tomorrow," replied Chip holding up the magazine he was reading and pointing to the guy blazing across the cover on a fluorescent pink mountain bike wearing a matching fluorescent jump suit, "Flash Freewheeling is making a public appearance at a bike shop downtown. I'm going to go and meet him."

"Oh no you're not," I replied, remembering how Coach D. chewed me out the last time Chip skipped the drills. "If you ditch practice I get nailed by the coach."

"You get in trouble because I skip practice?" mused Chip. "That's not fair."

"You're right it's not fair, but it's the way it is. I'm afraid you'll have to meet your mountain-biking buddy some other time."

"OK, I won't skip practice, then," Chip agreed, clutching his stomach and giving me a strange look. "But suddenly I feel too sick to play basketball. My stomach is killing me."

I smiled, catching onto Chip's plan. "With pizza like this, it's no wonder."

6

Fish and Chip

I was sweaty and tired when I stopped back at room 121 around noon the next day. The meal hall was serving something the guys were calling Mystery Meat Casserole, so I decided to put my stomach to the test with some of Chip's leftover pizza instead.

I had barely changed into a fresh T-shirt and taken a tentative nibble on a slice of pizza when there was a knock on the door.

"Who is it?"

"Is Chip there?" came a man's voice through the door.

"It's his parents," added a female voice.

I opened the door slowly, curious to see what sort of creatures raised the wacko who was sharing my room. When I opened the door I was surprised to see two very ordinary-looking people.

"Hello, I'm Chip's mother," said the woman, shaking my hand and walking right into the room. "You must be Jeff. Chip has told us all sorts of things about you."

I didn't like the sound of that, but I smiled anyway as Chip's parents wandered into the room and made themselves very much at home. Mrs. Carson was very tall and lean with long red hair and delicate features. Mr. Carson, on the other hand, was short and pudgy, and the only delicate thing about

him were the few strands of hair parted over the bald spot at
the back of his head.

Mrs. Carson smiled as she surveyed the mass of clutter
that filled the tiny room. "Look, honey. Chip is so much
neater when he's sharing a room with another boy."

"Yes, he sure is," Mr. Carson replied. He turned to me and
asked, "Is Chip around?"

"Um, I'm not sure," I said, tiptoeing around the potential
firecracker of a situation that was developing right under my
nose.

"Not sure?" echoed Mr. Carson.

"Is he all right?" said Chip's mother, furrowing her brow
and sounding worried.

Chip wasn't kidding when he said his parents were over-
protective, I thought, trying to decide how I should handle
this. Mr. and Mrs. Carson had shown up at the precise moment their son was out in the middle of the city looking for
some dude on a fluorescent pink mountain bike. What could I
say?

"Of course he's fine," I said, regaining my cool. "It's just
that Chip is so quiet that sometimes I'm not sure whether he's
here or not."

Mrs. Carson stared at me and looked suspiciously around
the tiny dorm room.

To escape her stare I got down on my knees and peered
under the bed. "Chip?" I called. "Guess he's not here," I said
finally, getting up and trying to look as casual as possible.

Mr. Carson surveyed the various bike helmets and tools
scattered around the room. "I wonder why Chip brought all
his biking stuff?" he wondered aloud.

"I wouldn't know," I said quickly. "He never really talks
about it much."

"Do you know where he is?" asked Chip's mother.

Yes, I felt like answering, he's out speeding down busy city highways on his bike about to become road-kill at any second. "He's at practice," I said finally.

"Practice?" she repeated.

"Why is he at practice and you're not?" asked Mr. Carson, cocking his head oddly.

Give me a break! There weren't this many questions on my final Social Studies exam.

"Because I'm injured," I said, growing alarmed at what a good liar I was becoming.

"Injured?"

"Ankle."

Suddenly their eyes were on my ankles, which of course looked perfectly fine.

"Shouldn't you have it strapped?" asked Mrs. Carson, bending down to get a closer look.

"No!" I jumped back. "It's an internal stress fracture ... third class on the fourth ... um ... tibia bone." I said, using the name of the only bone I could recall from biology class.

"The tibia is in your leg," corrected Mrs. Carson.

What was she? A doctor?

"She'd know," added Mr. Carson. "She's a doctor."

Just my luck.

"Whatever," I said, trying to hustle Chip's parents out of the room. "Anyway, I'll tell Chip you were here."

"We're going to be in the area, so tell him we'll drop by later this evening."

"Sure," I said, glad that my interrogation was over.

The Carsons were halfway out the door, when Mr. Carson poked his head back in.

"Come to think of it, maybe we'll just drop in on him at practice. Where's the gym?"

I choked on my tongue. "Um. You can't. I mean ... I'm not sure ..."

Chip's mother gave me a funny look.

"Not sure that that's a good idea," I recovered. "I mean, Coach D. is pretty tough. Yeah, real tough. One time this guy's mother showed up at practice and Coach got pretty ticked. Not to mention that everybody thinks he's a wimp now," I added under my breath.

She nodded and took one more look around the room. "Tell him we'll see him later today," she called as they turned to leave. "And stay off that ankle."

As soon as the door clicked shut I flopped on my bed and let out a huge sigh of relief.

"Chip Carson, you owe me," I muttered. "You owe me big."

***

I have never liked rebounding. I was never very good at it either. Big surprise there, being five foot two and not much of a leaper. Whenever I go up for a rebound the only thing I usually catch is somebody's elbow in my teeth. Spending an entire afternoon practice session learning to box out and bang the boards was not exactly my idea of a good time.

The drill was a tough one, too. Coach D. had us line up in pairs facing the basket. He would then heave the ball at the hoop and the two guys would have to battle for the rebound. I wasn't a very good rebounder in the first place, and the fact that I was lined up against Oak just made things worse. Every time the ball went up, he threw me away like a piece of litter and collected the rebound. If Coach D. hadn't been there yelling at us, I would have probably given up and started to dog it, but it was hard not to give it my all when Coach D. was watching.

"C'mon, men!" he bellowed, clanging another ball off the rim and watching two guys fight for it. "Go up and grab those boards. I want y'all to clean that glass like your name was Windex!"

As I got nearer to the head of the line I began to brace myself for another pounding when an idea struck me. I knew I couldn't overpower Oak, but I was a lot quicker than him.

This time when the ball went up, instead of trying to climb over the bulky boy when he boxed me out, I put my hand on his hip, and then spun around him and raced in to steal the ball before he could get to it.

"Nice play, son," said Coach D. as I flipped the ball to him and trotted to the end of the line.

"Sneaky," smiled Oak.

"Score one for the short guy," I laughed, slapping Oak's hand.

For the next couple of plays I had Oak totally off balance. When he thought I was going to zip around him I was able to step in front and block him out clean, but when he set himself for a good box-out that's when I would slip around and race in for the loose ball.

Using my unique technique I was able to hold my own banging the boards, and when the drill was over Coach D. strode over to me.

"Nice work, Lang," he said, clapping my shoulder. "I like to see a player who has some instincts for the game."

The lights could have gone out in the Dalplex right about then and no one would have noticed. My million-watt smile would have lit up the whole place.

***

When I got back to Howe Hall I found a worried Chip Carson pacing around the room.

"Man, I got busted, didn't I?" he said as soon as I entered.

"Busted?" I didn't understand.

"By my folks," Chip continued, getting a little freaked out. "They were here right? There was a message at the front desk. My folks were here — I wasn't — now I'm nailed. I may as well pack my stuff and brace myself for the mother of all parental lectures. I am toasted! Busted! Fried! Doomed!" Chip started thumping his head against the cement wall. Fortunately, he was still wearing his bike helmet, or else he could have hurt himself.

"Chip, let's focus, shall we?" I instructed, steering my unstable roommate away from the wall. "First, yes, your parents were here. Second, no, you're not doomed. I covered for you."

Chip looked at me like I was Santa Claus. "You what?"

"I covered for you, I told them you were at practice and that I was in the room because I was injured. They bought it; you're not fried."

"You ... covered ... not ... fried," he babbled deliriously, as finally it dawned on him. "Yes, guy!" Chip cheered, throwing my hands high in the air and then violently slamming a high-ten with his own. "Oh yes! You rule!" Chip whooped as he jumped on his bed and started playing a wicked air guitar. "What a team! I knew we would bond! This is too cool. You saved my life, Jeff!" Chip bounced off the bed, let out a few more thunderous whoops and furiously shook my hand. "This is the best. You covered for me? You rule. You covered for me!" He paused abruptly. "Why did you cover for me?"

I was wondering the same thing at the time. "I don't know, Chip. I just did, OK?"

"Definitely OK," Chip smiled and let out another ear-shattering cheer. "Most definitely OK."

I guess I really did know why I had covered for him. If there was anyone who knew what it was like to have parents drive you crazy it was me, and even if Chip was a bit loud and obnoxious, I didn't want him to get reemed by his folks.

"So, how was the legendary Flash Freewheeling?" I asked.

Chip shook his head. "You know when you think something is going to absolutely kick, and you're really up for it, and then it happens and it's lame and you feel like a big dolt? That's how I feel after meeting Flash."

"He was a jerk, huh?"

"Total," Chip shook his head. "Pro athletes just don't get it. Like, if it wasn't for us kids watching them, cheering for them and buying their T-shirts, they'd just be dumb jocks flipping burgers. But when we want an autograph they act like they're doing us the biggest favour in the world."

"Yeah," I replied, "it's just like—"

I was interrupted by a knock at the door. I opened it to reveal a scowling Tess Ward. Tess was wrapped in a white lab coat and had a pair of safety goggles dangling around her neck.

"Excuse me, I hate to bother you," she said in a tone that let me know she was actually quite happy to bother me, "but could you please not shout so much. Some people are trying to study."

"Yeah, like that freaky girl across the hall," called Chip, coming over and peeking out the doorway. "Oh. Sorry Tess."

She glared at him. "Just because your parents aren't here to keep you on a leash doesn't mean you can be totally uncouth."

"Duh, hey Chip, what does 'uncouth' mean?" I asked in my best dumb-guy voice.

"Uh, me not know," replied Chip. "Me not smart like Tess."

Chip and I broke out laughing as Tess shook her head and marched back to her room. She was almost there when she let out a terrifying shriek and Chip and I rushed out into the hallway.

"Oh no! Not more stink gas!" Chip groaned, watching in horror as a thin grey cloud floated out of Tess's room and started to spread out in the hallway.

"That doesn't look like gas," I said as the cloud drifted our way. It was only when it was upon us that I realized what had been unleashed from Tess's bedroom laboratory.

"They're bugs!" cried Chip, frantically waving his arms and running in small circles.

Sure enough, the grey cloud was made up of thousands of tiny flying insects buzzing through the hallway.

"Don't touch them!" shrieked Tess. "They're my fruit flies. I just bred a rare hybrid of fruit flies. I have to catch them."

"Catch them quick," advised Chip, rolling up a copy of *Mountain Biking Weekly*, "'cause in a second I'm going to start kicking some fruit-fly butt."

"This is too gross," I complained. "If you want a pet, get a cat."

"They're not pets, you moron," countered Tess, running out into the hall and squirting a clear solution into the air. "They're a unique scientific genetic experiment."

"That's what your parents said about you," mumbled Chip, waving his rolled-up magazine at some flies hovering near him.

"I took them out of their jar to count them. If you hadn't disturbed me, I would have been finished studying them before the sleeping solution wore off and this wouldn't have happened. If this experiment fails, I'm holding you personally responsible, Jeff Lang," Tess yelled, scooping some fruit flies up with a fine mesh net.

"Hold me responsible!" I couldn't believe it. "Whatever! Wait until the Department of Health finds out that you were breeding killer mosquitoes where people sleep!"

"They're harmless!"

Whack! Chip slammed his magazine against the wall, making fly pudding out of a handful of Tess's experiments. "They are now."

"Animal!" cried Tess.

Her shrieks were interrupted by the sound of a familiar voice floating down the hallway.

"Jeff, honey?"

Peering down the hallway I was less than impressed to see Sharon walking my way. I started to wonder if she had taken a course on bad timing or whether it just came naturally.

Before I could figure out how to deal with the Sharon factor, a chorus of voices in the other direction caught my ear.

"Chip? Chip darling, how are you?"

Sure enough, coming from the other end of the hall were Chip's parents.

Sharon, Chip's parents and a thousand fruit flies — I felt like I was in some ultra-bizarre sci-fi movie. What were the odds? Tess had managed to collect most of her fruit flies, but now Chip and I were about to get bugged some more.

"What do you say, partner," Chip said, grasping the hopelessness of the situation, "should we dive out the window, or hope that we're abducted by aliens?"

I just shook my head and waited for the inevitable.

Chip and I barely had time to brace ourselves before Sharon and Dr. Carson were kissing and hugging us.

I heard a giggle coming from across the hallway and broke from Sharon's embrace just in time to see Tess laughing at me. I gave her a mean look and slapped my hand against the wall, pretending to kill some more fruit flies. She winced, stomped into her room and slammed the door.

Back in my room, I introduced the Carsons to Sharon and, as luck would have it, they really hit it off. It turned out that Mr. Carson and my stepmom did the same sort of work and Dr. Carson was from the same hometown as Sharon.

Moving aside sweaty T-shirts and balled-up athletic socks, Sharon and the Carsons plopped themselves down in our room and started chatting away happily. They looked so comfortable I half expected them to ask me to serve them coffee and cake. No chance of that, the sooner they cleared out the better.

I started to get a little nervous, realizing that now I was the one in danger of being busted. If Dr. Carson asked me about my ankle, Sharon would freak.

Fortunately Mr. Carson's stomach put an end to my worry.

"Well," he said finally, "we best be getting some food into Chip, here. You know how much growing boys eat."

By the look of him, Mr. Carson obviously thought he still had some growing to do himself.

"You're going out to eat?" Sharon said, perking up. "Well, I have a fabulous idea. I'm hungry and Jeff must be famished. Wouldn't it be fun to all go out together?"

"Yeah, as much fun as juggling knives and chug-a-lugging a bucket of bleach," I mumbled.

"What a great idea," chimed Chip's mother, pretending not to hear my comment.

Chip and I looked at each other and groaned.

There was, however, no escape, and before I knew it we were piling into the Carsons' mini-van and cruising the city streets looking for — at Mr. Carson's request — a restaurant with an all-you-can-eat seafood buffet.

"Argh. Have ye ever been ta sea, Jeffrey," Mr. Carson boomed in a sea captain's voice as we pulled into the restaurant parking lot.

"Not without being sick," I deadpanned.

Sharon slapped me on the leg and shot me a "you-be-good" look. I wasn't hungry, but I bit my tongue anyway.

7

Mission Impossible

Ugh," grunted Chip, flopping down on his bed as soon as we got in the door, "that was harsh."

"What was? The seafood or the evening in general?"

"Both," groaned Chip. "Now you see what I meant when I said my folks were mental?"

"Your folks? Didn't you listen to Sharon going off all night?" I replied. "Don't talk to me about mental parents, because I've lived the adventure."

"I couldn't believe she talked for twenty minutes about how she organizes her purse," snickered Chip.

"Yeah, well at least she didn't start singing," I retorted.

Chip laughed out loud. "Leave it to my dad to pick the only seafood restaurant in the world that has karaoke."

"And then they wanted us to sing," I continued. "As if."

"Yeah, like it wasn't embarrassing enough watching them."

"Watching them twice," I cried. "Your dad went up twice!"

Chip grinned. "Yeah, Dad loves Elvis."

I tried not to laugh, but the image of the corpulent Mr. Carson howling and gyrating like Elvis was too much for me. "Hey Chip," I started to giggle.

"What?" he smiled.

"Your dad couldn't carry a tune in a backpack!"

It was all too much. The whole evening had been either super-tense or super-embarrassing and now, finally back in the safety of our room, we just lost it. Chip and I started howling with laughter. What had been the most unpleasant experience in the world two hours ago was suddenly hilarious.

For what seemed like an hour Chip and I were hysterical. After we finished making fun of the night's activities we started laughing at the other embarrassments our folks had put us through.

I told Chip about Sharon showing up at practice the other day, and he told me about his mom showing up at a school dance to get a picture of him dancing with his first date. I told him about Sharon coming into our locker room last season to deliver a clean pair of underwear before my basketball game, and Chip told me about his mom breaking out the naked baby pictures when he had a bunch of his friends over for a party.

Although these things drove us crazy at the time, hearing them out loud now was hilarious. Even though I thought Chip could have come from another planet, the embarrassment our folks put us through was one thing that we could both relate to.

"One time," Chip continued, rolling his eyes and giggling, "my dad was coaching my baseball team and he made me pitch even though I couldn't throw a baseball to save my life. So I was up there, trying to pitch, and I kept walking batters, and he kept telling me to 'find my rhythm,' and I walked another batter, and he kept telling me to 'find my rhythm,' and finally I had walked about ten guys in a row and they were smoking us seven to nothing and they hadn't even got a hit yet, and all the guys on the field were yelling at my dad 'he stinks, Coach,' and 'get him out of there, Coach.' My own teammates, man! They kept yelling at me and telling me I stunk and my dad just left me in and kept telling me to find my stupid rhythm." Chip had stopped laughing and his eyes looked grey. "Well, I never found it."

"Is that why you don't like playing team sports?" I said quietly.

Chip nodded his head. "It's not a lot of fun having your teammates telling you that you stink," Chip sighed.

"You don't, Chip," I said. "Not at basketball, at least. I know that. You're good."

"Yeah, whatever," Chip lowered his eyes. "I'm over it now, man. You don't have to try and make me feel good."

"I know that," I said, being honest, "and I still say you're good. I've played with you and you can play hoops. And you know, if you stopped worrying about making mistakes and just played the game you might actually have some fun."

Chip just shrugged.

"Really," I said flatly. "You're pretty good."

Chip looked at me seriously. "I can play hoops?" he asked, as if he couldn't quite believe it.

"Yes, you can play hoops."

Chip broke into a goofy grin. "That's cool," he laughed, "because man, do I ever stink at baseball!"

And with that Chip and I started laughing all over again.

                              ***

The next day Chip actually had his sneakers on and was ready to go to practice before I was out of bed.

"Jeff," he called, tapping the foot of my bed. "Jeff, we have a problem."

"Go away," I mumbled. I still had five minutes of shut-eye left, and the seafood from the night before had not settled well in my stomach.

"No, you really should check this out, man," Chip insisted.

"What is it?" I groaned, rolling out of bed and putting my foot down on the floor. It was wet. That was strange, I thought. Floors are generally not wet.

Seeing my surprised expression, Chip pointed at the door. "We're having a flood, man!"

Coming from under the door was a slow but steady trickle of water soaking the carpet.

"What the —" I exclaimed, trading puzzled looks with Chip. Then a single thought struck us.

"Tess," we cried in unison.

Sure enough, as we bolted into the hall we saw Tess trying unsuccessfully to stem a flow of water streaming from under her own door and into the hallway.

"What's going on Tess?" I asked, doing my best not to flip out on her.

"Nothing to be concerned about," she replied with a nervous laugh. "Just a little set-back with one of my tests."

"What are you testing?" challenged Chip. "An ark?"

"It was an experiment in hydroelectricity," Tess barked, losing her calm front. "Hydroelectricity, for your information, is using moving water to create electricity. It is a very important field and you'll just have to be patient while I correct this little problem."

"Little problem," yelled Chip, shaking his head as if he couldn't believe what he was hearing. "What do you mean 'little problem'? You're turning this place into Niagara Falls and you expect me to be patient! Who do I look like, Aquaman?" Chip fumed, splashing his foot in a puddle on the floor for emphasis. "I've had it. You know what, Miss Brain-a-Maniac, you're not as smart as you think you are, 'cause if you were you wouldn't always be ruining your experiments and ruining our lives."

And with that Chip waded back to our room and slammed the door, leaving me standing in the hallway with Tess in awkward silence.

***

"She is just too much," Chip said as we walked across the soccer field toward the Dalplex for practice. He was still fuming about Tess and I thought he might give himself a stress ulcer about the whole thing. It wasn't like Chip to get so worked up. "I mean, she thinks she's so great and just once I'd love to give her a taste of her own medicine."

"What are you saying, you're going to start doing science experiments?"

"Maybe," replied Chip with a gleam in his eye.

***

After the morning practice, Oak, Scott and I were scarfing down some soggy spaghetti in the dining hall. Well, Scott and I were eating; Oak had already finished his second helping and was now contemplating a third.

"I'm still hungry," the mountain of a boy sighed, "but if I have another serving I'll probably have a heart attack in practice."

Scott poked at one long strand of spaghetti and looked thoughtful for a second. "How come when it rains, earthworms always start crawling towards the road?" he asked no one in particular.

"Instinct," replied Oak.

"Pretty dumb instinct," mused Scott. "Like, do they all get together and say, 'hey fellas, it's raining, you guys feel like getting your guts squished out on the highway, too'?"

Oak put down his fork. "Thanks for killing my appetite, Scotty."

"I didn't think that was possible," I quipped.

"Hey, a growing boy needs to eat," replied Oak. "Besides, Coach D. likes my size."

"Oh, you mean he's not going to put you on the all-star squad because of your good looks and brains?" wisecracked Scott.

"Well, at least I've got a shot at making it," retorted Oak, punching Scott in the arm.

"Ow," exclaimed Scott, "that's my shooting arm. Coach D. won't pick me for sure if I'm not hitting my shots."

"Hit your shots? Scotty, you couldn't hit water if you fell out of a boat," laughed Oak.

We all started laughing and I wished I could relax about the all-star team the way Scott did. He just went out and had fun and, although he loved the game, he was realistic about his chances of making the team and didn't seem to put any pressure on himself. I, on the other hand, carried a brick around in my stomach and with every passing practice saw my chances of being selected for the rep team dwindle. There was only one scrimmage game left and if I didn't have a good game I could kiss any chance of making the all-star team goodbye. Apparently Oak saw things differently.

"Jeff, Coach still has his eye on you," he said.

"You think?" I needed all the assurance I could scrounge.

"Yeah, I doubt you'll start, but you definitely have a shot at second or third-string guard." I was eating this up. It's strange how when you want to hear something you really don't care who the source is. "But then again, Coach was giving that other short guy a hard look in practice."

"You mean Chip?" I asked, a little put off.

"Yeah, Coach likes the all-star team to play a tough full-court defence and he's always looking for quick guys who can come in like a spark plug and get the team going. Especially someone who can hustle and play the point ..." Oak continued his coaching analyses, but I had stopped listening and started worrying again.

This was wonderful. I had convinced my roommate to start playing hard, and now he was moving in on my spot on the all-star team. Something he didn't even care about.

***

When I got back to our room I was prepared to give Chip the cold shoulder, but the sight that met my eyes as I opened the door piqued my curiosity.

Chip was dressed like a cat burglar, wearing all black with a toque on his head. He was sitting in the middle of the floor staring intently at intricate maps, which were spread out before him.

"Chip, what are you doing?"

"Plotting our revenge," he responded with a strange look in his eye.

"Against Tess?"

"No, against the Klingons," he said sarcastically. "Of course, against Tess."

"It looks a little complex," I replied shakily, gesturing to the mass of papers spread over the floor.

"Oh, the maps are for the bike race on Thursday. Here's our revenge for Tess." He flipped me a spiral-ring notebook.

I started reading aloud. "Glass cutters, smoke bombs, infra-red goggles, grappling hook, plastic explosives." I stopped reading and gave Chip a worried glance. "Plastic explosives?"

"I couldn't get any plastic explosives," Chip mumbled.

"Grappling hook?"

"Um, actually I don't have any of that stuff," confessed Chip, "but if we did, we'd get her real good. I saw it in a movie once. This secret-agent guy scales the wall of the enemy fortress and plants plastic explosives all around the guard tower and then —"

"What's the plan, Chip?"

"Let's go over to her room, stick a tube of toothpaste under her door and stomp on it — *Splosh!*" Chip cried, slamming his foot down for emphasis. "Simple, yet effective."

I was a little hesitant. Sure, Tess was a pain, but I wasn't convinced that this was really necessary. "What if we get caught?" I asked.

"Caught?" Chip repeated, as if the thought had never occurred to him. "One, we won't get caught. Two, if we get caught, we just say we were doing an experiment with toothpaste."

"An experiment with toothpaste?"

"Yeah, we wanted to find out if it was a solid, liquid or gas and it got a little out of hand. Besides, after everything Dr. Frankenstein has put us through, surely a little toothpasting would only be fair."

I tried to protest, but it was hard to argue with that logic. It was even harder to find sympathy for Tess. "Let's do it," I said finally.

Chip smiled and tugged on his black toque, pulling down a full-face ski mask. "All right!" And with that, Chip grabbed an economy-size tube of toothpaste and slipped into the hallway humming the *Mission Impossible* theme song.

"Make sure no one is coming down the hall," Chip instructed. "I'll secure the stairs." From the precision of his commands I wondered if Chip had attended an espionage camp the previous summer.

Checking the end of the hall, I turned to give Chip an all-clear sign. I couldn't catch his attention, however, because he had stopped at the other end of the hall near the stairwell and was staring out the window.

"C'mon," I hissed, jogging to join him at the window. "Aren't we going to, you know ..." I made a squirting sound and pointed at the toothpaste.

Chip continued to stare thoughtfully out the window. Outside, the sun was beating down on the basketball court beside Howe Hall. On the court, a sweaty Jay Best was running drills by himself.

"No," Chip said finally. "I think I have a better idea."

8

One Last Shot

When I woke up the next morning, Chip was standing in the middle of the room wearing his spaceman/biking outfit.

"Another practice run?" I yawned.

"No more practices," replied Chip solemnly, adjusting his yellow visor, "no more planning, no more training. This is the real thing. I'm ready and now it's time for action."

"Are you going biking or joining the marines?"

Chip couldn't keep up his tough-guy routine. "I'm going to kick some booty!" he whooped, breaking into a wide grin and wheeling his bike out of the room. "I'll see you later, and don't worry, I fed Coach D. a line about going out with my parents, so he knows I won't be in practice."

That was ironic. Coach D. thought Chip would be out with his parents, and if his parents actually knew where he was, heads would roll.

"Hey, what's this?" Chip said, bending down to pick up a small folded piece of paper, which had been slipped under our door. Chip stared intently at the note for a moment before flipping it over to me. "What do you make of this?"

I sat up in bed and looked at the piece of paper. It looked like a fancy greeting card, folded over with the Dalhousie University crest on the outside. On the inside, written in flowing gold script was an invitation to the Dalhousie Faculty of Science summer program closing banquet which was going to be held the next night in the McInnis Room. The invitation was for Tess and had obviously been slipped under our door by mistake.

"Looks like a real high-class event," I said. "It says here that the head of the science department will be there along with all these other guys with really long titles."

"Maybe we should change the time on it or something," said Chip mischievously. "You know, just something to wreck her night."

I shook my head. "Spending a whole night in uptight clothes talking to old guys in suits about science: that sounds lousy enough to me already. Let her enjoy." I leaned out of bed and laid the invitation on top of my sneakers. "I'll slip it under her door before I go to practice."

"You do that," Chip said, wheeling his bike into the hall. "Anyway, it's race time. Wish me luck."

"Yeah," I yawned, "break a leg, man."

Chip gave me a funny look.

"What?" I shrugged. "It's a showbiz expression."

***

That morning's practice session was on jump shooting, so needless to say I breezed through it with ease. At the end of the drills, Coach D. even drifted over and mumbled something about my nice shots. Jump shooting was the one part of my game that didn't need encouragement. I spend so much time practising my shot that I could have practically given the clinic myself. For me there is nothing better than draining a smooth long-distance jumper. I wished we could practise shooting all day. Instead, I was sitting in the cafeteria trying to drain the not-so-smooth gravy from the meat and potatoes I had made the error of selecting for lunch.

"You know, I heard that they don't serve real meat here," Oak said, pointing at my plate. "It's just mushed up fishing bait and sawdust. That's why I always eat from the deli counter," he mumbled, gulping down the last few bites of a submarine sandwich roughly the size of an actual submarine.

"Yummy," I said with a grin, taking another bite and letting Oak know he'd have to do better than that to gross me out. "I'd go back for seconds except we have a game now."

Oak glanced at the large clock above the door. "Chill out, Jeff. We still have a few minutes. Besides, I do want to get seconds."

"Thirds," corrected Scott.

"What?"

"Thirds." Scott pointed at Oak's empty plate. "That was seconds."

Oak shrugged. "Whatever."

As Oak rushed back to the kitchen, Scott and I went to dump our trays. We were halfway to the garbage chute when Scott pointed across the meal hall.

"Hey Lang, isn't that your stepmom?"

It was funny, usually Scott spoke in a quiet voice, but he seemed to shout that comment as loud as the lead singer of Green Day.

Heads turned and the guys at a nearby table started whispering as, sure enough, across the meal hall Sharon was waving her arms, frantically trying to get my attention.

"Jeff, honey," she cried.

Turning red with embarrassment, I waved back quickly, hoping that she would quiet down. She did and took a seat at one of the long tables, removing her suit jacket.

"Hey there, darling," she said as I moved into earshot.

"Sharon, what's going on?" I hissed.

"Nothing," she said casually. "I didn't have anything on my schedule, so I came to see if I could interest you in some lunch. We could go to that Chinese place on Spring Garden Road."

"I can't do that," I said angrily. "I've got a game. I'm at basketball camp, remember? This isn't some family vacation."

"Oh well," my stepmom breezed, "it was just an idea."

"Sharon, don't you get it? I don't want you showing up here every day making me look like a loser. Can't you just stay away?"

"I don't know how I make you look like a loser, Jeff. I just thought it would be nice to spend some time together. After all, it was just a coincidence that we happened to be in Halifax at the same time, and there's only so much shopping even I can do. I don't see the problem if I pop by to say hello."

"There's no problem," I mumbled, feeling a little guilty for snapping at Sharon.

"Well, there obviously is," she said, clearly confused. "You sound very upset."

"Sharon, do you notice that of all these kids in here, I'm only the only one who's sitting with a parent?"

Sharon shrugged. "Well, maybe they would be if their parents were around."

"That's not the point," I continued. "It's just embarrassing, that's all."

Sharon looked a little hurt. "Well, I certainly didn't mean to embarrass you. If I had known I was so embarrassing I wouldn't have dropped by to see you. I thought maybe it would be fun, but obviously you're ashamed of me for some reason."

This was not going well. I was angry at Sharon for showing up, but it was so hard to explain why I didn't want to hang out with her in front of everyone. I guess I shouldn't have been embarrassed by her, but I was and just couldn't put the reason into words. Before I could think of something to say,

Sharon started putting on her jacket and getting ready to leave.

"Where are you going?" I asked stupidly.

"I'm leaving. Isn't that what you wanted?"

I sighed. "Sharon, I didn't mean it like that."

"Well, how did you mean it, Jeff?"

My stomach was twisted like a pretzel and I couldn't help wishing that Sharon would lower her voice so no one would hear our discussion. My mind was doing backflips trying to come up with a way to explain how I felt to her, but I came up empty. Besides, it was clear that I had hurt Sharon's feelings. It wasn't like I didn't want to talk to Sharon, I just didn't want to talk to her in front of all the guys. I was about to say that, but realized that she wouldn't understand it, so I really didn't have any choice but to back down.

"Sharon, look. I'm sorry, OK?"

"Sorry for being ashamed of me?" she said pointedly.

"No. For telling you not to come by. I'm sorry."

"That's OK," she said, standing up. "I still have to leave. I think I have a meeting."

I watched Sharon walk off with mixed amounts of relief and guilt. The feelings of relief quickly disappeared and left me feeling like the biggest ungrateful brat in the world.

"Hey Lang," Oak called as he walked out the door with Scott. "You coming to practice with us, or did you want to go with her so she could hold your hand?"

"Shut up, Oak!" I hollered amidst scattered laughter. "Hey guys, wait up!"

***

There are times when I just don't buy the old saying, "It's only a game." As I tightened the laces on my sneakers before the scrimmage game that afternoon, I decided that this was one of those times. It was my team's last scrimmage at the camp, which meant that this was my last shot to show Coach D. what I could do in a game situation.

Of course, it wasn't just my last chance to impress Coach D., it was my teammates' last shot too, and everyone knew it. I guess that was why everyone was tight-lipped and quiet before the game. Everyone, that is, except for Jay Best. Jay was talkative and friendly, even chatting with a few guys from the other team before practising some tricky turn-around jump shots. Much to my disgust, he made most of them.

I know it sounds selfish for me to wish that Jay was off his game, but just watching him lope around the court, flipping in difficult shots like they were nothing made me fume. Besides, he was a sure bet to make the all-star team anyway, so why couldn't he just let someone else shine for once?

That was wishful thinking. After the tip off, I watched Jay strip the ball from the opposing guard and accelerate down court for a layup which would make any highlight reel. It was clear that Jay was as up for the game as the rest of us, maybe even more. It was as if he kicked into a higher gear that the rest of us just didn't have.

It took a few plays before my team stopped standing around watching Jay and started playing together. Jay had already scored our first eight points, but we were only up by two.

The team we were playing was ranked below us in the standings, but they were still giving us a run for our money. Their best player was the same guy with the pony-tail who had tried to make me look bad during a pick-up game a few days earlier. They also had a few big guys who were pretty deadly in the low post.

I had drawn the defensive assignment of guarding the guy with the pony-tail, and he was taking it to me. Although I could probably guard him one-on-one, his teammates were always springing him loose by setting baseline screens for him. I was just too small to fight through the picks and that left him free to rain jump shots on my head.

"Keep hustling, Jeff," Jay called as the guy with the ponytail drained another jumper.

"Yeah, whatever," I grumbled. I was getting a little frustrated, and Jay's encouragement wasn't about to help.

On the next possession, Jay pushed the ball up court and zipped a pass to me on the wing. Although my defender was stuck to me like gum, I launched a jump shot anyway. It was a bad shot, and I knew it. The ball clanged off the back of the rim.

"Let's work it around a bit," Jay called, racing up and putting pressure on the ball carrier. The small guard tried to bull his way past Jay, who neatly stole the ball at half court and started leading the fast break the other way.

It looked as if Jay was going to take it all the way himself so I parked myself under the basket on the off chance that he missed. At the last second, however, Jay fired a bullet pass my way. I wasn't expecting the pass, but I did manage to catch it — right in my face.

The ball smacked into my nose and sent me reeling. It felt like my nose was swelling to the size of a melon and the last thing I saw before my eyes teared over was Jay snatching the loose ball and powering it in for a layup.

Seeing that I was injured, the ref blew the whistle and helped me off the court.

"Sorry about that, Jeff," Jay said sincerely, as one of the guys handed me an ice pack. "It was a bad pass."

"Doe pwob-lem," I said, holding my nose. Everyone knew it was a great pass, and if I was any kind of ballplayer I would have caught it.

"Well at least Jay scored the hoop," observed Oak. "Since it bounced off Jeff's face, does he get the assist on that?"

Everyone started laughing and I felt like an idiot.

"Well, your nose isn't bleeding," Donovan said finally, peeking under the ice pack. "Why don't you have a sit down, anyway."

The ref blew the whistle and play resumed. I just sat on the bench and seethed. I continued to sit there as Jay Best tore up the court, making fantastic shots and unbelievable passes. Despite his efforts, however, the other team just wouldn't go away. When I finally got off the bench at half-time, the score was knotted at thirty. Donovan wasn't happy about the first half at all, and he let us know it in the huddle.

"Lazy, lazy, lazy play!" he boomed. "I want to see some hustle out there. Oak, you've got four fouls. Play smart defence and move your feet. I want all of you to crash the boards. Don't wait for gravity to bring the ball down to you, go up in the air and get it."

Donovan instructed us to start the second half in a full-court trap that we had just learned the other day. Even though not all the guys knew exactly how to play the defence, the strategy disrupted the other team's rhythm. In the first ten minutes of the second half they had more turnovers than a French pastry shop.

Although the team was getting into a groove, I was struggling. I managed to make a few baskets, but I was still forcing my shots and getting beat on defence.

The next time down the court, Jay swung the ball over to me as I spotted up at the elbow of the key. The tough guy with the pony-tail crouched low and glared at me.

"C'mon, take it to me, punk," he sneered.

Taking him up on his challenge, I tried to fake left and drive right, but I shuffled my feet and the ref called me for travelling.

"Next time pack a suitcase, loser," the pony-tail guy growled. I gave him a nasty look as the ref gave the other team the ball.

Falling back into a half-court man-to-man defence, I set myself in front of the pony-tail guy and denied him the ball. He wasn't about to sit still, though, and as he made his cut through the key along the baseline I was blindsided by a pick set by one of the big men. A step behind, all I could do was rush at the pony-tail guy as he got the ball and nailed a short jump shot.

"In your face," he snarled, slapping hands with one of his teammates.

On the next time-out Donovan was barking out instructions. "You guys have to tighten up on defence. We got to challenge every shot they take. No easy hoops!" He clapped his hands for emphasis.

"Hey, Jeff," Jay piped up. "How about I give you a rest on defence and guard the shooter with the pony-tail for a while?"

Donovan nodded. "That's a good idea, Jay. You and Jeff switch on defence."

I nodded and bit my lip. It was true I was having a tough time, but I hated being told to switch off. It was like letting everyone know that I couldn't do the job. I glared at Jay.

With Jay smothering the hot-shooting pony-tail guy on defence, our team was able to put together a run and open up a lead. With only a few minutes left, it looked like we were coasting to victory when Oak got whistled for his fifth foul. With our big man on the bench, the tide turned pretty fast. Without Oak's muscle in the middle, the other team's forwards could set up camp in the post and grab all the rebounds. We suddenly had a tough time getting anything going.

Coming down the court, I called for the ball and nailed a twenty-foot jumper, letting it fly just over the fingertips of the guy with the pony-tail. I glared at him, but decided against talking any trash.

With only twenty seconds to play, they were still up by one and we called a time out.

"Still lots of time, guys," Donovan assured us as we huddled around. Since we didn't have any set plays for this situation, Donovan just encouraged us to work the ball around, set lots of screens and look for a good shot. He did make one call, though; he told Jay to handle the basketball.

As Jay brought the ball up court, the other team was putting on a lot of defensive pressure. The guy defending me was practically climbing inside my jersey as he denied me the ball. Jay waited patiently at the top of the key, sizing up the situation. I made a hard cut through the key as one of our forwards set a screen for me, knocking off my defender and leaving me wide open about ten feet from the hoop.

"I'm open!" I shouted, clapping my hands and calling for the ball.

Jay looked my way and then, ignoring me, drove hard to the hoop. Dodging traffic like a squirrel on the highway, Jay made a great spin move in the lane to shake off the defence. Then, taking two great strides, the muscular boy powered himself to the hoop before getting clobbered from behind by the guy with the pony-tail.

The final buzzer sounded just as the ref blew his whistle for a foul. There was no time left, but Jay would have two free throws for a chance to win the game.

As Jay stepped to line to shoot his foul shots, I couldn't help but think that I had been wide open on that play and would have made the winning shot. I guess it didn't matter now, because Jay was in the process of stroking two perfect free throws to win the game. Everyone crowded around him and started cheering and clapping. Coach D. went over to shake his hand, and I was left standing near the outskirts of the celebration, half-heartedly shaking hands with my teammates.

I had blown my last chance to impress Coach D. Without a doubt, Jay was the hero, and I was left with nothing but a sore nose and a badly bruised ego.

**

Trudging along the sidewalk towards Howe Hall I spotted a large, shiny trophy coming down the sidewalk towards me. The trophy had a golden cyclist on the top and a grinning Chip Carson attached to the bottom.

"That doesn't look like one of those dinky everyone-who-participates-gets-a-trophy trophies," I said as Chip wheeled his bike into earshot.

"No way, slick." Chip grinned proudly, waving his trophy. "I placed first in my division."

"Congratulations," I said, trying to be cheerful.

"Say, what's wrong with you? Something happen at your game?"

I guess I wouldn't make a good actor.

"No. Same old thing. I play my guts out only to be shown up by Jay Best," I said, my frustration boiling over. "Just once I'd like to see that guy screw up. You know, just so he knows what it's like to feel like an idiot."

Chip let out a little laugh. "Not so loud, Jeff, here comes the superstar now." Chip nodded across the lawn. "You want me to whack his kneecaps with my trophy?"

I laughed. "No thanks."

The white knight was walking down the sidewalk a little distance behind me. To my surprise, Jay didn't walk right into Howe Hall, but rather detoured to talk to Chip and me.

"Hey Jeff, great game," he said, extending his hand.

"Thanks," I replied, slapping five with the soon-to-be starting guard on the Nova Scotia Juvenile All-Star team. "Nice shooting." I tried not to grimace.

"Thanks," Jay said breezily. "I shoot two hundred foul shots every day. I guess making two in a game isn't that big a deal." Jay paused awkwardly before lowering his voice and continuing. "Say Jeff, can you do me a favour?"

I raised my eyebrows. "Depends what it is." The way I was feeling, unless Jay was looking for someone to slam his head in a door, he was probably going to be out of luck.

Jay gave a nervous laugh. "Well, I've been thinking about what you said, and I think I'd rather if you introduced me to Tess."

I tried my best to smother a laugh and let out a strange wheezing sound instead.

"Asthma acting up, huh?" Chip covered.

"Yeah," I gurgled, trying to keep a straight face. "You know, Jay, I really don't think that's a good idea —"

"Sure it is," Chip interrupted.

"It is?" I didn't believe what I was hearing.

Jay looked admiringly at Chip. "You know Tess, too?"

"Oh yeah, we go way back," Chip said confidently.

"Would you introduce me?"

"Well, I would. But I'm just not sure if you're her type."

"Type?" Jay and I asked in unison.

Chip shot me a sly look. "Yeah, Jeff, you know the guys Tess likes: rugged, tough guys. Good-looking rebels who play by their own set of rules."

"I can be a rebel," Jay said quickly.

Chip looked Jay up and down. "Well, she might go for you. She'll play hard to get, that's for sure. So you can't give up."

Jay nodded excitedly.

"Plus, you'll have to show her you're a real jock. You know, flex your muscles, mess up your hair and have that scent of cheap cologne with just a hint of sweat."

"No problem," Jay said.

Chip looked unconvinced. "Well, I'm still not sure. Let me think about it, and maybe I'll set something up."

"That's all I can ask." Jay beamed, thanked us and hurried off.

I turned to Chip. "Did the wire connecting your brain to your mouth get knocked loose on the bike race? What are you saying?"

Chip waved his hand. "Quiet please, I'm working on a plan."

9

Acting Like an Adult

In the dim light of a desk lamp, Chip and I were relaxing in our room. I was lying on my bed, and Chip had cleared off a space at his desk where he had been furiously writing for the last twenty minutes.

"Chip?" There was no answer. "Hey, Chip!"

Chip's head popped up, and he plucked the headphones off his ears. "Did you say something?"

"I was just wondering, Chip. How did you get your bike here without your folks finding out in the first place?"

Chip looked at me like I was the dumbest guy on the planet. "I took it apart and packed it in my suitcases," he replied.

"Right."

Chip shook his head and went back to writing. A few moments later his head popped up again.

"Jeff?"

"Yeah."

"Do you spell 'goddess' with one 'd' or two?"

"Two. Why?"

Chip went back to writing. "No reason."

"What are you writing over there?" I asked, kicking my sneakers onto the floor. "A novel?"

"Well, we wouldn't want Jay to meet his sweetheart without a letter of introduction. Would we?"

"You're sending Tess a letter?"

"Not from me," Chip corrected. "From Jay. How do you spell 'infatuation'?"

"I don't know."

"Doesn't matter, I'll use 'got the hots for you' instead." Chip scratched a few more lines and then finished his work with a flourish. Folding it carefully, he flipped it onto my bed.

"Go slip that under Tess's door, would ya?"

"Why me?"

"We're a team, aren't we? If I'm going to be the creative genius, you can at least help with the leg work."

"What if she catches me?"

"There you go with that 'getting caught' stuff again," Chip said, waving his hand dismissively. "Keep that up and you'll have an ulcer by the time you're twenty."

"Well, it's just that —"

"Forget it," interrupted Chip. "If it's such a big deal I'll do it myself."

"All right," I caved in. "I'll do it."

Chip beamed.

Stepping into the hallway, I immediately saw that getting the letter under Tess's door was impossible. Mainly because Tess was right in front of her room. She was crouched in her doorway, attaching a piece of cardboard along the bottom of her door with duct tape.

"What are you doing, Tess?" I asked, neatly tucking the note away in my pocket. "Preparing for another flood?"

Tess clicked her tongue. "If you must know, I'm preparing an experiment involving photoelectrics, radioactivity and nuclear particle momentum. I have to put this cardboard along the base of my door in order to prevent light from getting in and disturbing my experiment. It's very important work and I must gather and analyze my data before this evening."

"Why? Is that when we can expect the nuclear melt-down?"

Tess sighed. "No. That is when I am attending the closing banquet for my science program. The head of the science faculty will be there, and if this experiment proves what I suspect it will prove, then I will have some findings that will impress the valence electrons off of him." Tess let out a little laugh at her science joke.

"Right," I said, drifting back towards my room. "Well, you have fun."

Tess gave me a superior look and resumed her work.

"Mission accomplished?" asked Chip as I entered the room and shut the door.

"No can do," I replied, explaining how Tess was out in the hallway preparing for another experiment.

"Oh well," Chip shrugged, "I guess two love letters will have to do."

"Two?"

"Yeah, I slipped them under her door this afternoon. Although this last one was a dandy."

"I'm sure it was," I said shaking my head. "Say, it's a good thing I gave her that party invitation, though," I continued, "she's really excited about showing her stuff to some head science dude."

"Poor guy," said Chip, looking up from a biking magazine. "If Tess is going to be around, I suggest he wear a wet suit, a gas mask and plenty of fly repellent."

"That's probably standard dress at these mad scientist banquets," I laughed. "A hundred science fanatics all waiting for Tess to tell them about her great experiment and then blow the place up. Too bad Jay Best couldn't be there. I'm sure if he saw her in full-force science-action he'd love her even more."

A thoughtful expression crossed Chip's face as he closed his magazine. "That's not a bad idea," he mused quietly.

***

Coach D. was running us hard during the last practice of the week. He made us do endless wind sprints, tough full-court layup drills and killer defensive drills where you crouch down and shuffle side to side until you think your back is on fire. The funny thing was, it didn't really bother me. After two whole weeks of tough games and practices I was in better shape and I was a better player. I guess that was a big part of the reason why I came to the camp in the first place.

"OK men, gather round," called Coach D., taking a perch on the bleachers at the far end of the gym. "I just wanted to take this opportunity to tell you how much of an improvement each and every one of you has made this week. You should all be very proud of your accomplishments. Give yourself a big hand." Coach D. paused as we all clapped and cheered.

"Now, tomorrow morning there will be a brief assembly in the dining hall. I will announce the names of the twelve boys I would like to be on the Nova Scotia Juvenile All-Star team. After the assembly I will give each of the team members an information package explaining everything you need to know about the all-star team and the tournament next month.

"Once again, thank you for all your hard work and I'll see you tomorrow."

A buzz went up from the campers as we broke away and started leaving the gym.

As Chip and I neared the door, an anxious Jay Best hustled up to us.

"Hey guys," he called. "You know, I don't want to be a pest, but I just wondering, when ... or if ... you know ... when you could introduce me to ... Tess."

My mind started steaming, trying to come up with some excuse why this would be impossible. Unfortunately Chip opened his mouth first.

"No problem, Jay," he said cheerfully. "Jeff and I have been talking you up. The thing is, she's really busy with all her science projects and stuff."

Jay looked downcast.

"But," Chip said, "she does have this reception thing tonight in the McInnis Room. It starts around seven, so why don't you stop by and show her your stuff?"

"Are you sure it's OK to meet her at this reception?" Jay looked a little worried. "I mean, I wasn't invited. Is it polite to just show up?"

"See Jay," Chip put his hand on Jay's shoulder, "that's exactly what I'm talking about. If you want to impress a woman like Tess, you can't be worried about being polite. You have to be a powder keg of passion, exploding into a mass of manliness and sweeping her off her feet."

Jay looked a little sceptical, but Chip barrelled on.

"Now, remember," he said, clapping Jay's shoulder, "you're a man. You're tough. You're a rebel. So show up tonight and show her your stuff. She'll definitely play hard to get, but you play your cards right and she'll be yours, pal."

Jay nodded and thanked us once again before hurrying off. He was headed no doubt to do some extra layup drills or something.

"Have you lost your mind?" I hissed at Chip. "Where exactly are we going to be this evening when Jay crashes Tess's science gala extravaganza?"

"I don't know about you, but I'm going to be right there watching," Chip replied, flashing a wicked grin.

I laughed most of the way back to our room.

10

A Not-So-Blind Date

Why do people say 'you can't have your cake and eat it too'?"

"It's just an expression, Scotty," replied Oak.

"It's doesn't make a lot of sense, does it?" continued Scott. "I mean, why would you want cake if you can't eat it?" The keen observation came in the middle of a high-stakes penny poker game that Scott, Oak and I were playing in the second-floor lounge.

"Like, what else is cake good for?"

"It's just an expression, Scotty," Oak repeated. "Now would you deal the cards?"

"Can you build things out of cake? No. No one ever said, 'give me some cake, I'm not going to eat it, I'm just going to build a house.' A cake house wouldn't be any good."

"You're starting to sound like my grandfather, Scott," I said. "Deal."

"It just makes you wonder, doesn't it?" Scott paused, shook his head and starting dealing the cards.

Oak jammed a fistful of potato chips into his mouth and examined his cards carefully. "So at last count, there are only two spots remaining on the Nova Scotia Juvenile All-Star team," Oak stated grandly.

"Really," Scott asked, getting excited. "What positions are still up?"

"Coach D. hasn't decided on a second-string guard or a backup power forward."

"So?" I asked expectantly, looking intently at Oak.

"So what?" asked Oak, discarding three cards and then looking like he wished he hadn't.

"So did I make the squad?"

"Well, Jeff," Oak said, furrowing his brow, chewing thoughtfully and making a bet, "I'm afraid my sources are a bit fuzzy on that issue."

I was confused. "But you're sure two spots are still open?"

"I'm sure."

"So that means you're sure ten spots are filled."

"I'm sure."

"So am I one of those ten guys?"

"I'm not sure."

"I call," Scott chimed in, throwing another two pennies into the pot.

A thought suddenly struck me, and at the risk of having my face rearranged I decided to say what was on my mind. "Oak?" I said bravely.

"Yeah?"

"You're full of it."

Instead of breaking my arms as I half expected, the giant boy just grinned. "Probably," he said, finally laying down his cards. "Can anyone beat a pair of two's?"

"Three jacks," I said. Scott and I started laughing and I raked in the sixteen-cent pot.

I was still smiling as I started dealing another hand when a figure near the stairway caught my eye. It was Sharon. She wasn't waving or yelling "yoo-hoo," she was just standing there waiting for me to notice her. From the way Scott, Oak and I were sitting, only I could see her, and I had no idea how long she had been standing there.

I played the next hand as quickly as I could and then excused myself from the game.

"How long have you been there?" I asked as Sharon and I walked down the hall.

"Not that long. Look, Jeff, if you're free for a bit I thought maybe I could treat you to dinner." She added quickly, "If you can't, I understand."

I half laughed. "Yeah, dinner sounds good."

"Great."

Sharon and I walked to the exit in awkward silence. I knew I had to say something to make up for the other day, but I was really at a loss for where to begin.

We were in the car and halfway to the restaurant before I even dared to bring it up.

"Hey, Sharon."

"Yes," she replied expectantly.

"Um, I'm sorry about the other day."

"Sorry why?"

She wasn't about to make this easy for me.

"Sorry for making you think I'm ashamed of you. I'm not. I mean, you're pretty cool. For a stepmom and all, that is."

Sharon wrinkled her brow. "Thanks. I think."

"It's just that, I guess, sometimes people my age like to believe we're totally independent. You know, all grown up. Which I know I'm not, or at least, I hope I'm not because you're still three inches taller than me, and it would really stink if I don't get any bigger."

Sharon laughed.

"So, even though it really shouldn't be a big deal, it was just hard for me to feel comfortable talking to you when I was the only guy there who had a parent around, you know, the only guy who still looked like a kid. Does that make any sense?"

"A little," Sharon gave me a warm look. "And I'm sorry too."

"How come?" Heck, I could drag this out too.

"For not backing off and understanding that you're at an age when you want to be grown up, and, Jeff, you almost are grown up. I mean you're a young man. I should have seen that and respected that." She reached over and gave my arm a squeeze.

"Thanks, Sharon," I said, giving her a sly look. "Say, since I'm so grown up and all, you want me to drive for a bit?"

"Fat chance."

***

"I can't believe we're doing this," I said to Chip as we hustled across the Dalhousie campus.

"Are you kidding?" replied Chip. "Thanks to us, Jay Best is about to meet the girl of his dreams. Don't you think we should be there for the special moment?"

"Not that," I hissed, hauling open the huge hardwood door that led into the foyer of the large stone building that housed the McInnis Room. "It's just these disguises are a little ... um ..."

"Ingenious?" offered Chip.

"Unnecessary," I corrected.

"Hey, if you want to go to a science banquet, you got to dress the part."

Dressing the part meant that we were outfitted for maximum nerdiness. We were both wearing black-rimmed glasses with short-sleeved white dress shirts and grey flannel pants. To complete the look Chip and I had slicked back our hair with the ultra-cheap hair product, Ick-O-Gel ("Maximum Ick for maximum stick!" the jar proudly proclaimed).

After Chip had finished geeking us out I was sure we looked more like photocopier repairmen than science campers. "Couldn't we just peek through a door or something?" I whined as I pulled on the leg of my trousers. The pants were so short I considered having a party to invite my pantlegs down to meet my ankles.

"No way, Jeff," Chip scoffed. "When Jay Best gets shot down there's only one place I want to be. Front row, watching the whole thing in living technicolour and true-to-life stereo surround sound." Chip flashed a wicked grin. "We should have brought popcorn."

"Do you really think he's going to show?" I asked as we trotted down a long arched marble corridor.

"Absolutely," Chip said confidently. "I went down to see him about an hour ago."

"You what?"

"Just some last-minute coaching, you know, telling him to be cool, to be macho, not to worry about Tess playing hard to get — nothing serious," Chip assured me.

"Did he say he'd come?"

"For sure, buddy," Chip said knowingly. "He thinks he's picking Tess up to go to a movie with him."

"You told him Tess wants to go out with him?" I asked, wide-eyed.

"Of course," Chip replied matter-of-factly. "I wouldn't make us dress up like Super-Nerd and Geek-Man if it wasn't one-hundred-percent guaranteed that Jay was going to show." Chip tried to look hurt. "Give me some credit."

I silently agreed that I'd underestimated Chip. After all, you really shouldn't put anything past someone who brings Ick-O-Gel to basketball camp.

Turning a tight corner, Chip and I found ourselves standing at the entrance of a grand conference room. Inside were long tables elegantly set with white tablecloths and sumptuous-looking plates of appetizers. A large banner hanging over a podium at one end of the room read, "Congratulations Science Explorers." In the middle of the room a mixture of young people and older important-looking men and women were chatting, while white-suited caterers mingled about serving finger food.

"Wow," I let out a low whistle, "nice — hey!" A wave of panic washed over me as I saw Chip wander into the large conference room.

"We can't come in here," I hissed, catching up to him just inside the large set of double doors.

"We just did," replied Chip, casually reaching out and plucking a chicken skewer from a nearby tray of appetizers. "Besides, wasn't that the plan?"

"I don't have a plan," I said, starting to sweat as I realized we were surrounded by very serious, very smart science types who probably wouldn't be amused by the idea of unleashing a love-sick jock on their little soirée. "You have the plan, remember?"

Chip was unflappable. "I know, so keep cool, would you?" he mumbled with his mouth full. "You know, these things are pretty good ... could be a bit more tangy, though ..." He waved the chicken skewer around thoughtfully. "Excuse me," Chip called out to a penguin-suited waiter, "do you have any salsa?"

I started to roll my eyes, but the sight of a familiar figure stopped me cold. My stomach did a backflip. "Chip, there's Tess!" I hissed.

Across the room Tess had cornered a distinguished-looking gentleman behind a table of hors d'oeuvres. She was yakking his ear off and he, understandably, was looking very bored.

The man had a grey beard and spectacles perched on the end of his nose. He looked like every scientist in every movie ever made. He also looked as if he was going to doze off at any moment. Chip and I wandered nearer so we could eavesdrop on the conversation.

"... really, Professor Schultz, I just have to say how brilliant I thought your paper on atomic particle acceleration was," Tess gushed.

"Um, yes," mumbled the professor, making a step to the left and trying to squeeze between Tess and the hors d'oeuvre table. "Now, if you'll excuse —"

"And may I add that it's wonderful for you to be supporting the fabulous summer science program here at the university," Tess rambled, making a move to block the professor's departure.

"She plays better defence than I do," I snorted.

"Borrrrring," Chip sang out, adjusting his black-rimmed glasses and glancing at his watch. "Jay won't be here for another ten minutes. I'm going to snag some more finger food."

"Yeah, feel free to make yourself at home," I called, chasing after Chip as he zeroed in on a tray of eats.

We had only taken a few steps when something across the room caught Chip's attention. "Wow! Check it out!"

Chip's eyes lit up as he looked towards the far end of the conference room where some science campers were showing off their super-ambitious projects. One display contained detailed information on animal intelligence and another showcased lasers; further down it appeared one girl had dedicated her entire life to studying ocean tides. Despite these impressive displays with colourful charts, graphs and fully functioning models, Chip was gawking at a booth showing energy-efficient methods of transportation.

In front of the booth was a strange-looking vehicle. It had two wheels and was set low to the ground with an aerodynamic metallic nose cone and a single seat in the rear. Despite its futuristic design, Chip instantly recognized what it was.

"Hey, man," he called, approaching the smallish science student who was displaying the project. "Cool bike!"

The short young man, who was dressed exactly like Chip and me in a short-sleeved white shirt and grey flannel pants, gave us a condescending glance. "Actually, it's a prototype H.P.G.T."

Chip furrowed his brow. "Could I buy a vowel, please?"

The boy chuckled. "The H.P.G.T. That stands for Human-Powered Ground Transport."

Chip didn't blink. "That's what I said: cool bike."

"It's actually designed for city transportation as an environmentally friendly alternative to cars or buses. You'll notice that it has a specially designed cockpit with extra storage space in the back as well as—"

"Mind if I sit in it?" Chip interrupted, already climbing into the contraption.

"Um, I'd rather you—"

"Hey, pal," Chip called, examining the mechanics of the super-bike as he submerged himself in the cockpit, "your brake pads are on backwards."

The young scientist stiffened. "The H.P.G.T. has a beryllium frame, carbon-fibre tri-spoke kevlar wheels and a sophisticated gear mechanism."

"Yeah, but your brake pads are on backwards," Chip repeated, popping his head out. "And your front derailleur is on wrong."

"You must be mistaken," came the short reply. "Now kindly get out of the H.P.G.T."

Chip whipped a bike wrench from his breast pocket, "Hey, I'm already in here, man," he breezed casually. "I may as well fix your bike for you."

Without hesitation, Chip set to work, unscrewing parts, pulling brake cables and leaving the sputtering inventor bug-eyed and speechless.

"Don't worry," I said, trying to reassure him. "He's pretty good with bikes."

A minute later the bike surgeon was finished. "All right," he cried triumphantly, propping himself up in the driver's seat, "this puppy should roast now. Here, I couldn't quite figure out where these should go." Chip sheepishly handed the science student a few screws and some small metal parts. "Say, you don't mind if I test it out?"

"No! You really can't!" yelled the student, getting quite alarmed.

"Sure, just over there," Chip said calmly, pointing to the other end of the display booths. "There's plenty of room."

Apparently, Chip was better with brake pads than he was with steering because his powerful piston legs had barely started pumping before he managed to plow the nose cone of the sleek vehicle into the side of the display booth.

The super-bike was unscathed, but the display was wobbling like a seasick tourist.

Chip bounced out of the cockpit of the vehicle and surveyed the wreckage. Unruffled, he turned to the stunned science camper. "Yeah," he said, "brakes are OK. If you want, I'll take a look at that little steering glitch—"

I grabbed Chip by his arm and hauled him away from the accident scene as fast as I could. "Way to keep a low profile," I said sarcastically. "Next time let's just run around naked shooting off fireworks."

"Hey," Chip bristled, "don't blame me for an obvious design fault."

"There's an obvious design fault in your head," I retorted.

"All right, I'm sorry," Chip replied. "Now let's go grab some eats."

"Forget it," I said, coming to my senses, "let's get out of here before—"

"Before Jay gets here?" Chip cut in.

"Exactly."

Chip grinned. "Too late. He's here."

I winced as I noticed Jay Best strutting across the room. Sporting designer mirrored sunglasses perched on his nose, he was stylishly dressed in an expensive nylon track suit and shiny white athletic shoes.

"The sunglasses were my idea," Chip said as Jay homed in on his love target. "Nice touch, no?"

I couldn't reply. I was holding my breath.

As Jay strutted towards Tess, people couldn't help but do a double take. With practically every other guy there dressed in a short-sleeved white shirt and grey flannels, Jay looked very out of place.

"Oh man," I said, finally able to speak. "He sticks out like a ... like a ... I don't know what."

"Like a jock in a roomful of science geeks?" Chip aptly suggested.

"Exactly."

As Jay swaggered through the room he paused for a moment near Chip and me. "Hey, Jeff," he called. "I didn't know you wore glasses. They look good."

Jay strutted away and I shot a glance at Chip. "Great disguises."

"Hey, don't blame me," Chip whispered. "Clark Kent puts on a pair of glasses and nobody can figure out he's Superman. At least we changed our hair, too."

Tess was just saying goodbye to the professor when Jay approached her. Chip and I quickly moved into earshot and got ready to watch the fireworks.

"Hey, Tess," Jay called, whipping of his sunglasses in a dramatic fashion. "I'm here."

Tess turned and looked him up and down. "Congratulations," she replied in a voice so frosty it could have been served at Dairy Queen. "And you are …?"

Jay flashed his perfect braces-free teeth through a crooked smile. "I think you know who I am," he crooned smoother than maple syrup on butterscotch pudding. "I'm Jay Best." He stretched out the *ay* in Jay and spat out the *t* in Best so it sounded like "J-a-a-a-a-y Best-ta."

There was a long pause as Tess said nothing and glared at Jay and Jay said nothing and grinned at Tess.

"You're pretty good at brainwashing people," I whispered to Chip. "Especially for a guy with no brain."

"No talk. Show time," Chip said briskly. "Oh my, it can't be," he cried, pushing his way up to Jay and Tess. "It is. You're Jay Best, aren't you?"

Jay nodded slightly, looking suspiciously at the nerdy Chip.

"I'm Theodore Goreham," Chip gushed, furiously shaking Jay's hand, "I think you're brilliant." Chip turned to Tess. "This guy is absolutely brilliant."

Tess stared at my roommate strangely. "Chip, what are you doing here? And why are you dressed like that?" she asked pointedly.

Chip was unfazed. "Never mind that, now. I'm trying to introduce you to Jay Best. He's one of the greatest young scientists in the country."

Tess looked confused. "What do you mean?"

"What do I mean?" Chip cried as if he couldn't believe his ears. "I mean this guy is easily the smartest guy in the room. I can't believe you've never heard of Jay Best. What do you do? Spend all your time locked in your room doing little experiments?" Chip laughed at his ironic joke. "Jay Best has won the Governor General's Award for Science the last two years. The scores on his Nova Scotia achievement tests were so high they had to change the marking system. His paper on astral physics was recognized by the Canadian Astronomy Association and as if that wasn't enough for a sixteen year old, he's going to spend the rest of the summer working as an assistant in the chem lab at the University of Toronto!" Chip turned back to Jay. "Jay Best, I am honoured to meet you. Let me just say that everyone in my chess club thinks you're the greatest!"

Tess was visibly impressed by the credentials Chip had just laid out. Heck, Albert Einstein would have been impressed by that résumé. "Is that true?" she asked, looking at Jay with a new-found respect.

"Of course not," Jay growled, snatching defeat from the jaws of victory. He glared at Chip. "What are you talking about?"

"And he's modest, too," Chip continued.

"I'm no academic nut. I'm one hundred percent jock," Jay declared, thrusting his chest out proudly.

"Right," Chip laughed. "But congratulations on winning the Canadian Junior Science Fair. I've never seen a robot like that before."

"That's garbage. Tess, I did win Basketball Nova Scotia's MVP Award this year."

"Such a good sense of humour. Jay also went to the Science Olympics and won the solar-car design competition."

"Liar!" challenged Jay, "I went to provincials in track and field and placed first in the high jump and third in the 400-metre dash." He looked beseechingly at Chip and me.

Chip kept rambling, "At the county chess meet, Jay won the championship game in only twelve moves."

"Only eggheads play chess!" countered Jay, turning red. "But Tess, I can bench-press one hundred and twenty kilograms." And with that Jay unzipped his nylon jacket and started flexing his chest muscles.

"Oh my God," Tess said with disgust. "You're a pig."

"What can I say?" Jay purred. "I'm a real man."

"Are you insane?" Tess cried, raising her voice. "I've had enough of this nonsense. Now, I don't know who you are or what you're doing here, but please, this is no place for a Mr. Universe competition."

A few of Tess's science buddies perked up at the sound of her tirade and stared at Jay. I'll hand it to him, Jay was still trying to play it cool but he looked as if he had all the confidence of a man addressing a stadium full of people with his fly down.

"But I thought you said —"

Before Jay had a chance to give the game away, one of the science campers pushed his way through the crowd and stepped between Tess and Jay. The guy barely came up to Jay's chin and was even shorter than Tess. He was wearing the standard white shirt with grey pants, and his small squinty eyes were magnified by thick glasses. I recognized him in a flash. He was the poor guy whose super-bike Chip had taken out for a test spin.

"Is there a problem here, Tess?" he said tentatively.

Tess rolled her eyes and forcibly moved her friend to one side. "Terence, what are you doing?"

"Just rushing to your aid, my darling," he declared grandly.

Tess wasn't impressed. "Your darling?" she echoed in disbelief. "How many times have I told you that we will not use cutesy terms of endearment in this relationship? I do not belong to you and I will not be referred to in the possessive."

Terence took the scolding to heart and muttered an apology. However, he remained standing in front of Jay with a defiant look on his face.

Jay looked confused. "Are you two together … I mean is she your …?"

Terence nodded. "That's right. Tess is my girlfriend." Terence caught a glare from Tess and realized his mistake. "I mean, Tess is *a* girlfriend, um, to me. She belongs to no one, obviously, but as an independent woman of the nineties she sometimes allows our affections to be mutually shared."

Tess beamed. I felt sick.

"We didn't plan on this," I hissed.

"Who cares?" Chip whispered back, grinning like an idiot. "I told Jay she'd play hard to get. Tess has a boyfriend. How much harder to get is there than that?"

Jay was obviously thinking along the same lines as Chip. "Hey Tess, let's stop these little games and get going," he said flashing a grin and trying to be smooth.

"She's not going anywhere," Terence boomed, puffing out his chest like a pint-sized peacock. Catching a look from Tess, he backpeddled furiously. "I mean, if she wants to, of course, she can. Me, not being in a position to speak for her, I can't say. But I get the distinct impression that she doesn't want to go anywhere. Right, Tess?"

"Of course not. Now, would you be quiet," snapped Tess, silencing Terence before he challenged Jay to a slide-ruler duel. Then a look of recognition dawned on her face. "Did you say your name was Jay Best?" she said slowly, a connection apparently fusing together in her brain.

Jay nodded and cracked a wide smile, glad that Tess was familiar with him after all.

"You're the nut who keeps sending me those embarrassing letters."

"Letters?" Jay swallowed his smile.

"Oh, don't play dumb with me."

Jay wasn't playing. "What letters are you talking about?"

"Those horribly immature love letters. They were full of bad poetry and references to me as the 'gardener of love.'"

"Um, I think that's the 'goddess of love,'" Chip corrected quietly.

"Whatever," Tess shot back dismissively. "His handwriting is very poor, too."

"Look, Tess, I really don't have a clue what you're talking about," Jay replied, clearly stumped. "The fact is, you agreed to go out to a movie with me tonight. Now are we going or what?"

"Of course we're not going!" Tess practically shouted. "And I never said any such thing. I would never date a muscle-bound, sports-crazy, athletic supporter like you. Whatever gave you such a ridiculous idea?" Tess cried, trying desperately to keep control.

"They did!" Jay wailed, pointing towards Chip and me. He was too late, however. Chip was already hauling me away from the fray.

"Well, it's getting late," Chip called, hurrying towards the exit. "Thanks for the fabulous time. Good food and fun was had by all. Must do it again next year. Bye bye!" He broke into a trot as we neared the doors. "Let's get out of here," he hissed. "Quick!"

I broke into fits of laughter, and by the time Chip and I raced out the doors we were both howling. We didn't stop laughing until we were safely back in our room, tucked into bed with the door locked and braced by several heavy pieces of furniture.

"That was classic," I said finally.

"Yes," Chip said, flashing me a thumbs-up sign. "On the Chip-o-meter that scam rated a solid nine point five. Well done, partner."

I laughed and switched off the light. "Well done, yourself," I replied.

Chip let out another little laugh and settled in between the sheets. "Yes, I am the king."

Camp All-Star

Blinding sunlight streamed through the window of room 121 when I woke up on the last day of camp. I was anxious to get to the morning assembly, where Coach D. would announce the all-star team. I closed my eyes and thought back to all the good shots and nice plays I had made in the last couple of weeks. Running the Jeff Lang highlight reel in my head made me feel better about my chances of making the team. I capped off the highlight reel by imagining Coach D. calling my name. It couldn't hurt to think positively.

Although I thought I had woken up early, Chip was already dressed and lying on his bed, his legs bouncing to tunes pouring into his ears through his headphones.

As I gazed around the room I figured Chip hadn't got up before me; he'd just stayed up all night. He must have because our room — previously known as the Chip Carson Toxic Waste Disposal Site — was amazingly clean. It was as if all of Chip's clothes, stereo equipment, magazines, CDs, biking gear and his bike itself had been magically sucked into two large suitcases which were now set in the middle of the room.

"It's blue."

"What's that?" asked Chip, seeing that I was awake and removing his headphones.

"The carpet. It's blue. It's the first time I've seen it."

"No one likes a wise guy, Jeff," cracked Chip, whizzing a pillow at me. "I think my stuff packed away quite nicely, except for that stupid trophy." Chip pointed to his prized mountain-biking trophy, which was placed carefully between the two suitcases. "It just wouldn't fit. I hope my folks don't ask about it."

"If they do, I'm sure you'll find some way to explain it."

"Oh yeah, no doubt," Chip said confidently. "It just bugs me that I had everything all figured out so they'd never suspect a thing and then I go and ruin my plans by winning a stupid trophy."

"Maybe you should just tell them the truth," I replied. "Who knows, they might be proud of you."

Chip gave me an odd look. "You think so?"

"They should be," I said, hauling myself out of bed and starting to stuff balled-up sweat socks and smelly T-shirts into my duffle bag.

After I finished most of my packing, Chip and I made our way over to the dining hall for Coach D.'s assembly. Chip wasn't exactly excited about the idea of sitting through another one of Coach D.'s speeches, but I dragged him along anyway.

The dining hall was packed as we entered a few minutes before the coach was about to speak. Freshly showered and wearing clean clothes, all the guys were packed into long rows of chairs facing a makeshift podium. The room was buzzing as campers discussed which twelve lucky players they thought would be selected for the all-star squad.

I scanned the crowd for familiar faces. Without messy hair and gym gear, it was hard to recognize the guys. Finally I spotted Oak and Scott sitting near the front of the hall. Oak was loudly making predictions about the team's roster while Scott marked down Oak's picks in a notebook. Noticing me, Oak gave me a big wave and then flashed a thumbs-up sign.

"Looks good for you, Lang!" he called. Scott nodded and gestured for me and Chip to come sit next to him.

I smiled and shook my head. Instead, Chip and I settled for seats near the middle of the cafeteria. "Hey, there's the Love Machine," said Chip, laughing and pointing at Jay Best, who was sitting a few rows ahead of us. "Hey Jay! How's Tess?" he shouted, waving and giving Jay a big grin.

Jay glared at us for a long moment before turning to stare at nothing in particular with a smug expression on his face.

I guess Jay could afford to look a little smug. It was a lock that he had made the all-star team. My own chances, I thought, weren't quite as secure. Realistically, I couldn't say things looked good. Besides being one of the smaller guys at the camp, I was also one of the youngest. On the other hand, aside from that last league game and the first couple of practices, I did play fairly well for the two weeks.

Despite my efforts to be realistic, my hopes were soaring. Face facts: I had dreamed about making the Nova Scotia Juvenile All-Star team ever since I got the camp brochure a couple of months ago. It would be great to tell my dad, Sharon and all the guys back home that I made the special squad and would be going to a huge tournament in Ontario.

All my reasoning and rationalizing ended as Coach D. stepped to the podium and cleared his throat.

"Here we go," I whispered to Chip.

Chip made no reply. He was plugged into his headphones and his eyes were closed.

"Gentlemen," Coach D. said, "I would first like to say that it was an honour and a privilege to work with you fine young men over the past two weeks. Each one of you has made tremendous advancements in your skills on the basketball court, and I hope you have also learned the importance of teamwork and sportsmanship. Because that is what I like to believe this camp is all about."

Coach D. paused as all two hundred campers broke out into wild cheering and applause. Even though I suspected Coach D. gave this same speech every year, the man was so dignified that I couldn't help but bristle with pride at being part of his camp.

"This camp should really be called Camp All-Star because each and every one of you young men has distinguished himself. For the amount of sweat and effort you put forth over the past fourteen days you all deserve a spot on this special team. Unfortunately, I am only able to choose twelve extraordinary players to represent this province as part of the Nova Scotia Juvenile All-Star team."

Coach D. then produced a sheet of paper from his shirt pocket and cleared his throat. I know it's corny to say it, but I was tingling with excitement. It was as if Coach D. was calling out lottery numbers and I had good odds of having a lucky ticket.

As Coach D. rhymed out names I kept track of the number of spots left by counting down on my fingers.

"Marcus Johnson ... Richie Sutherland ... John Girodat ..."

There were still nine spots left.

"Sundeep Singh ... Jay Best ..."

I shot a quick glance at Jay, who was nodding his head quietly in triumph.

Coach D. called out two more names. Five spots left. I closed one hand into a fist.

"Rick Calapari ..."

I noticed the thick pony-tail guy slap five with a guy sitting next to him.

Four spots.

Another two names were called. I could see boys give small cries of celebration as their names were announced. I felt my stomach twisting a little as I realized I was down to only two more spots.

"Trevor Sparks and Gary Lynch."

I closed my other hand into a fist and let both hands fall into my lap.

I had not made the team.

I held my breath for a moment, half expecting Coach D. to return to the podium and say something like, "Whoops, silly me! I forgot to call out Jeff Lang, who also made the team." Of course, it didn't happen.

I turned to say something to Chip, but my roommate was blissfully grooving to his tunes, probably unaware that Coach D. had said anything at all.

As the room began to empty I sat quietly for a moment and let out a big sigh. I was disappointed like you wouldn't believe. It didn't help that Jay Best went out of his way to walk right in front of me and deliver a meaningful glare.

It took me another moment before I noticed that no one else was sitting down looking at their shoes. In fact practically everyone — even the guys who didn't make the team — were talking and laughing. Scott Tran was laughing so hard that he had to lean on Oak for support.

"Great inside information," he cried, laughing at Oak, who hadn't made the team, either. "Way to pick 'em, Oakie!"

"So I was a little off in the predictions this year," Oak smiled sheepishly. The bulk of a boy broke out laughing and play punched Scott.

I lightened up a little and went over to help Scott razz Oak. In a few minutes we were all laughing and chatting.

When we finally wandered out of the cafeteria, none of us was even talking about the all-star team, least of all Chip, who was still plugged into his portable CD player, humming tunelessly to himself.

***

As my two-week basketball adventure drew to a close, Chip and I locked up room 121 for the last time and dragged our luggage down to the front drive.

We were waiting only a minute before Chip's parents pulled up in their blue mini-van.

"Here," I said, taking one of Chip's suitcases, "I'll help you load the van."

"Thanks,"

I had moved only a few steps with Chip's luggage when Chip's mom rushed up to me.

"Jeff, let me take that," she said, taking the suitcase. "You shouldn't put any strain on your ankle."

"Why? Oh, right," I said, remembering my injury. "Thanks, Dr. Carson."

We were still loading Chip's stuff when Sharon came to get me. Of course, she started chatting with the Carsons and gave them our address and invited them for dinner and all that stuff, while Chip and I just kicked the dirt and waited.

"Well, I guess this is it, man," I said, shaking Chip's hand firmly.

"Yeah," said Chip, "I guess it is. It was fun, huh?"

"Yeah," I said. "Take it easy."

"Yeah. You too." Chip opened the back door of the mini-van. "Hey Jeff," he called.

"Yeah?"

"See ya next year."

"See ya next year," I laughed. "Roomie."

Chip hopped into the van, but before the door closed I could hear Mr. Carson say, "Nice trophy, son. Why's there a biker on it?"

"Well, Dad," came Chip's muffled voice, "funny thing about that ..."

"Ready to go?" Sharon asked.

"Ready," I said.

"Hey, Jeff, you want to drive?"

I gave her a look.

"I'm just kidding," she said.

We both laughed, got into the car and cruised down the tree-lined street towards the highway.

I was surprised that I was in such a good mood. After all, I had been hoping like crazy that I would be picked for that all-star team. Don't get me wrong, I was disappointed, but even though I didn't make the team, I wasn't writing off the whole camp as a failure. After all, I was one of the youngest guys at the camp and also one of the smallest, and I had still played well and had a great time.

I thought about the events of the past fourteen days; about Chip and Jay and Tess and Coach D. and everything I'd learned — both on and off the court. I had to smile. The two weeks weren't exactly what I had expected. But then again, things seldom are, I guess. Besides, next summer I would be another year older and another year taller. I was already excited about coming back.